THE ROOM TO THE WEST

LAUREN BIEL

This is a work of fiction. Names, characters, events, and incidents are the products of the author's imagination. Any resemblance to actual persons, living or dead, or actual events is purely coincidental.

ISBN: 979-8-9855002-1-9

Library of Congress Cataloging-in-Publication Data

The Room to the West/Lauren Biel 1st ed.

Printed in the United States of America

Cover Design: Pretty In Ink Creations

Content Editing: Sugar Free Editing

Interior Design: Sugar Free Editing

For more information on this book and the author, visit: www.LaurenBiel.com

This book depicts strong sexual content, sexual assault, substance use, and violence. This story also contains themes of suicide. Read at your own discretion.

For the family I lost before they ever got to see me publish my first novel

CHAPTER ONE

I hold a lighter to the end of a cigarette dangling between my lips. My red lipstick is smudged. The water runs in the bathroom, the sound smothered by the flick of my lighter. The tip of the cigarette lights up and sizzles, and I inhale the smoke into my lungs. The bathroom door closes, and he appears at the foot of the bed—a nameless form. He pulls on his jeans and buckles his belt as he walks beside the bed and puts three one-hundred-dollar bills on the nightstand. He reaches out a hand and brushes my cheek.

"I'll be in touch, Hannah."

Hannah. The way he says my name disgusts me, as if the pleasure still hangs on his tongue.

I nod at him, and he closes the hotel room door behind him as he leaves. The cigarette hangs from my lips as I crawl out of the cheap bed and grab my clothes. The soft fabric of my dress drapes my skin as I pull it over my head and smooth it down over my hips.

I don't enjoy this lifestyle, but I also don't hate it. I pick the clients I'm willing to sleep with, and each one has some

1

redeeming quality. One may be old but fiercely intelligent. One may be ugly but extremely generous. This lifestyle allows me to break away from the typical nine-to-five grind. My friends in college struggle with schoolwork after working all day at dead-end jobs, and all I have to do is play a certain role for an hour or two. It's not a bad gig if you're willing to sell your soul a bit.

I am.

Hannah. That's the best name I could come up with because I'm not exotic or unique. The only unique thing about me is that I'm the slightest bit overweight for an escort. Only two clients know my real name is Mariah. They know my name and that the money they give me goes right into my college tuition fund. I'm not doing this for luxuries or to get high; I want to become a teacher one day. Hopefully my students never learn that to get in front of them, I had to get beneath too many men.

I'll leave this hotel and head home to my apartment, where I'll fill the parts of my soul I've given away with liquor and Xanax. Every client leaves with a small part of me tucked into their pocket, and I'm not sure what happens to me when I've given every piece away. I have nothing—even with what's left of me—to give to a man that may deserve it. Not that I have the time or the desire to date, anyway.

There's no point trying to find love. I can't give them those feelings in return. I'm incapable of such reciprocity. You can't peel away your flesh until you're nothing more than a skeleton and expect someone to love your bare bones.

As I step outside, I let the hotel door close behind me, and I'm wrapped in the warm Arizona air. Even though I moved here a year ago, I still haven't gotten used to these temperatures in the summer. I came from Upstate New York, where cold and snow blankets the ground half the year.

I drop my cigarette on the ground and squelch it with the

toe of my high heel before getting into my car. Even my clients tell me to quit, so I know it's a bad habit. Little do they know, the cigarettes help mask the taste of them in my mouth. I prefer the burnt chemical residue over the salt of their sweat. The nicotine crawls into my brain and numbs my racing thoughts.

I make the short drive home and flip on the light as I step into my apartment. The fabric of my dress falls as I walk into the bedroom; I never let my clothes from these nights follow me here. It's my safe place.

I walk into the bathroom and turn the shower on. The cold marble countertop gives me goosebumps as I wait for the shower to steam. My reflection in the mirror stares back at me. My makeup is smeared, and my messy hair falls out of the ponytail. Fog creeps over the mirror and washes away my reflection.

I climb into the shower with a sigh and let the hot water fall over my body. My head drops backward, and I try to wash away the filth of tonight. That's one thing my friends at their desk jobs never have to do. Not every night, at least. I wash over some bruised skin on my chest and around my nipples, flinching slightly.

Rarely do they pay to make love to you.

MY PHONE CHIMES AND WAKES ME UP, ALERTING ME to a new email. I roll over and look at the clock on my nightstand. It's late morning. The email's subject line reads "Looking for an evening." Several pictures are included. The first is of an older man wearing a jacket over a turtleneck shirt. He looks to be near seventy, if not older, and he makes me think of a college professor. The picture looks like it was professionally taken. The next few pictures are of his home. It's gorgeous. The front is nearly all glass windows that reflect the sun back at the photographer.

I finish scanning through the pictures before turning my attention to the body of the email.

Hello, Hannah. I hope my greeting finds you well. I saw your pictures online and wanted to extend an invitation to a night in my home. My dining table has been empty for a while now, and I would love an opportunity to prepare a meal for you and enjoy your company, if that suits you. If you would like to set up a date, please send a message in return.

I don't like going to clients' homes. It's not because I worry about being murdered—they can do that easily enough in a hotel room, and they won't have a mess to clean up afterward. It's because most clients' homes are filled with pictures of their families.

Photographs and children's drawings cover every surface. The images portray a wife who's smiling because she's blissfully unaware her husband is fingering me beside the very table her photo sits on. I will grip the same areas of the blanket where her hands have grasped in pleasure. If they have sex at all, that is. I will grab a drink out of a fridge whose doors are cluttered with children's paintings and school projects.

It's the most intolerable part of this job; I'm assisting a husband with an affair. Some escorts take pride in "saving" marriages with their services. They help men to remain in their celibate marriages by putting out when their wives won't. I find nothing honorable about it, but I try to rationalize. If it wasn't with me, it would be with some other woman, and at least I give a shit about destroying their families.

I may bend my rule for this client. I send a reply asking

for a day and time that would work for him. It doesn't take long before he responds with his address and a time for our date.

Tonight?

I open the date book from beside my bed and look for today's date. August eighth. I think I can pull it together for tonight, so I tell him I'll be there at six.

It takes a long time to prepare for a night out like this. I stand in front of the mirror and use a curling wand to form ringlets in my dark hair. The styled locks graze my shoulders. Black eyeliner traces my hazel eyes to make them look larger. Mascara stretches and fills my eyelashes. They nearly touch the lenses of the glasses perched on the bridge of my thin nose. I've showered and shaved every inch of my body already. I pull on a red dress that stops just below the curve of my ass. Deep red lipstick is the finishing touch to my look.

I cover my outfit with a long, lightweight jacket, trying to hide my profession from anyone who isn't my client. I slip on black heels, turn off my apartment lights, and close the door behind me.

I PULL UP TO THE HOME AND STEP OUT OF MY CAR. The house is beautiful and probably one of the biggest I've ever been to. My heels click against the marble walkway leading to the door. I let my hands brush against the flowers and well-groomed shrubs dotting the pathway. A woman must live here, based on how incredible this landscape looks.

I sigh and knock gently at the door.

The intercom hums to life. "I'll be right down!" says a voice from the speaker.

Silence again.

The locks click and clack as they're undone. The chain of yet another lock rattles away from behind the door. Every so often in this job, I question if today will be the day I end up chained in someone's basement. I look back at my car as the door eases open. It's too late now.

"Hello, Hannah. I'm Thomas." He reaches a shaky hand out to me.

I take it in mine and smile at him. He moves aside to let me in, and I step onto stark-white tile floors. The house looks like something out of a magazine, and I look like something . . . well, out of a magazine, but a much more intimate one.

He helps me out of my jacket and hangs it on a hook by the door. "If you wouldn't mind taking off your shoes." He motions toward a mat he keeps near the entryway.

I slip off my heels and place them next to a pair of men's running shoes and a couple pairs of dress shoes. I don't see anything to indicate a wife resides here, after all.

Thomas ushers me toward his kitchen, and I look around in painfully obvious admiration. It's beautiful and something I couldn't afford in my entire life, no matter how many clients I took on.

"Come, come sit." His voice is low, calm, and comforting. Again, I get the idea that he is—or has been—a professor. He slides a chair out from the table, and I sit down. He smiles at me as he lifts the metal cloche from the silver serving tray. I didn't even know people used those in real life.

"I cooked salmon. I hope that's alright with you."

I nod in response. He sits down and places the folded napkin over his lap, picks up the fork and knife, and cuts into his food. I do the same.

"You're very beautiful, Hannah. How old are you, anyway?"

"I'm twenty." I blush because I don't take compliments well.

"Oh my. I have grandkids your age." He laughs nervously and wipes his mouth. "I'm sorry. I don't do this."

"Do what?" I ask as I cross my legs.

"Pay for . . . company. It's just been really lonely since my wife passed away." He takes a drink before continuing. "She died of cancer nine months back, and I've been alone in our home ever since. We moved away from our children and grandchildren to retire here several years ago." He clears his throat as if fighting back tears.

"What made you email me?" I ask, trying to change the subject.

"It's funny, actually. It's how well your profile was written. You seem articulate and intelligent." He says this with an excited lift of his eyebrows.

I'm likely the first escort whose intellect has been praised as her most alluring feature, and I don't know if I should be offended or not.

"Why, thank you. I'm starting my second year of college," I say. I use the napkin to dab my face so I don't smear my makeup. I push the plate away, my nerves tensing my stomach too much to eat further.

"Oh, you're a student?" His eyes light up. He stands, pulls a box off the counter, and slides it toward me.

He shifts his weight with excitement as I pull off the cardboard lid and put it to the side. After digging through the tissue paper, the red-and-black plaid of a schoolgirl outfit emerges. His gaze meets mine. I'm now ninety percent sure he's a professor. He smiles at me and urges me to go put it on with nothing more than his eyes and a quick nod.

"Where's your bathroom?" I ask with an uneasy feeling in my stomach.

He motions down the hall and to the left. My bare feet

patter on the cold white tile. I flip on the light in the bathroom. It's huge—almost as big as my entire apartment. I stand in front of the double marble sinks and look at myself in the mirror, trying to remind myself it's just a part I have to play.

Think of it as when a secretary has to put on their whole "customer service" façade.

I undo my dress and stand in front of the full-length mirror as the fabric falls past my silky black panties. They're covered again by the thick and itchy material of the plaid skirt, the bottom of which cuts off at mid-thigh. I pull the white button-up shirt from the box and slip my arms into it. It doesn't quite fit, and my breasts create gaps between the straining buttons. My black bra is visible beneath the thin, cheap material of the shirt. I slip the black stockings up over my knees.

I take a breath before walking back into the hallway. Thomas sits in a leather armchair in his living room. His leg is crossed over his lap, and he's drinking a dark liquor. Probably bourbon. He seems like a bourbon man. He looks at me and removes his glasses before setting them down on the table next to him.

"Hello, Hannah. Thank you for meeting me in my office," he says, completely in character. Even his voice sounds different. The sternness of it catches me off guard, and I feel guilty for whatever make believe thing I was supposed to have done.

"Okay," I say uncomfortably. My voice is strained and too high. I never said I was a good actress.

Thomas stands up and points to an identical armchair next to his. "Please, come sit."

I walk over and sit beside him. The leather rubs against my skin as my skirt rides up my thighs. He sits back down but turns his body toward me. The hardened anticipation in the crotch of his slacks leaves no question of his intentions.

"I know you've worked hard this semester, but I have to fail you on that project you submitted yesterday. It was clearly plagiarized. I was surprised to see such a bright and ambitious student produce such poor-quality work on this final assignment."

His expression and this conversation are so authentic, I'm certain he's reliving a fantasy. Some young girl sat in his office, hearing those exact words at some point in his career. He doesn't seem like the type to act on it in the moment. Perhaps he crossed his legs to hide his excitement as he scolded her. Maybe he thought twice because he didn't want to lose his wife or his prestigious career. Regardless of the reason, he wants to reenact it with me tonight.

It's not even close to the weirdest fantasy I've helped recreate.

"Please don't fail me. I've worked so hard this semester! I just didn't have time to do this assignment. Please?" I fall into character. My voice is pleading and panicked. I've been here before, begging for a redo on an assignment as an F dangles in front of me, threatening to ruin my GPA.

"You could have asked me for an extension, you know. There's no excuse for this." His voice is stern, and he looks down at me with genuine disappointment in his eyes.

I stand up and crawl between his legs, looking up at him with doe eyes. "Surely there's something I can do to pass the course?" My glasses have slipped slightly down my nose. I bite my lip.

He looks like he's thinking about my proposition, almost as if this isn't going quite how he fantasized. Nonetheless, he stands and unzips his slacks before removing them and folding them on the table beside him. He isn't wearing underwear, so he just stands in front of me, fully erect. I'm taken aback, having figured him as the kind of guy who wears tighty-whities.

"I think we could make an arrangement," he says with a soft, sultry tone.

I smile up at him and take him into my mouth. He smells clean, like bar soap. He drops his head back and grabs the back of my head, thrusting his hips into my face and smearing my lipstick. Usually, this is their favorite part, but he ends this faster than I anticipated. His excitement is palpable as he motions me to my feet. He pulls me into him and grabs my ass with two cold, shaky hands. He turns me around and buries his face into my neck, sniffing deeply.

A lot of men do that.

He groans into my neck before bending me over the arm of the chair, his hands creeping up my skirt and crumpling it above my waist. He reaches a hand back and slaps my ass, checking my reaction for consent to keep going. When I nod, he continues.

Not a lot of men do that.

He hits me again and plays with himself against my skin before pulling a condom out of the pocket of his shirt. The wrapper rustles as he tears it open, and the scent of latex fills my nose. There are always several moments of awkwardness during this part. I feel like I should ask if they want me to do it for them, but I never do. While I wait, my mind wanders.

Did I forget to lock my door at home?

Usually, their prying hands pawing between my legs brings me back to the now. No matter how experienced or aged the man is, they never seem to be able to do this part smoothly. They end up poking and prodding, and Thomas is no different. I finally reach back and help him by guiding him into me. Once he's inside, he groans, and I moan with him. The sound is half plastic.

Thomas likes fast, shallow thrusts, and he mumbles to me

about my assignment. I'm not particularly listening. He only wants me bent over the chair. Maybe he wants to see her face instead of mine.

The leather creaks as he thrusts rhythmically until he slows and groans as he comes. He pulls out, and I stand up. We proceed to the second most awkward part of this; I stand there naked or half-naked while they wrestle the condom off a limp noodle and try to find somewhere to throw it out.

Thomas leaves me alone in the den. The crackling of the fireplace soothes me, even though my skin is still flushed with heat. He comes back into the room in a fuzzy white robe. I've replaced the costume with my dress—the soft fabric is much more comfortable—and I hand him the folded outfit. He tucks it under his arm. I slip my jacket over my dress and carry my shoes in one hand. He opens his wallet and rifles through it, pulling out much more than we agreed upon. He hands it over to me. I look down and see at least ten one-hundred-dollar bills.

"Oh no, I can't take this. This is too much." I try to hand back the large set of bills, as much as it pains me to do so. The money burns and embeds itself into my hands.

"No, I want you to take it. I didn't mention the outfit when I emailed you. It's only fair to compensate you for the additional time and effort." He pushes my hand away.

I smile up at him, lean over, and kiss his cheek.

He reaches out and wraps me up in his arms. "Thank you," he whispers, and it almost seems like he's going to cry. Instead, he pulls away from me and smiles.

I stare at him for a moment. He has soft, wrinkled features and dark but kind eyes. He's quite a handsome older gentleman. I don't typically take notice of my clients' faces, as I prefer most of them to remain faceless, but he's a unicorn client.

"Well, thank you. You can message me anytime, Thomas.

It was wonderful meeting you," I say as I head for my car. I only peeled back a single layer of myself tonight. I'm still recognizable.

Every so often, you get a wonderful client like Thomas, who doesn't make this job seem so bad. There are some clients I don't feel I need to wash off immediately. Maybe we could have been friends in a different life, bonding over a cup of coffee instead of our bodies. There are not enough of these clients.

CHAPTER TWO

Many of my clients are pump-n-dumps. I don't know a damn thing about them aside from what their dicks look like. I could meet them in the street and not even recognize them. They recognize me, though, and will usher their lovely wives in the other direction.

Most of my clients have deranged and taboo fetishes. I've been asked to pretend I was their children's babysitter, taken against her will. They would pin me down and force themselves on me in an act of dubious consent. The tears were real as they pounded against me, confrontational words spewing from their lips.

I've been asked to play someone barely legal and sometimes, even younger than that.

Some men love to choke me to the point of unconsciousness, their hands wrapped so firmly around my throat, I wondered if I would wake up as blackness blanketed me. The grunt that escaped their lips as they shook me would be a final memory. Whenever I came to, they would be on me, fucking me when I could neither protest nor consent.

These men hope to use my body to fulfill their deepest, darkest fantasies, and for the right amount of cash, I'll allow it.

I've allowed myself to be punched, cut, beaten, and humiliated for money. Men will open their wallets wider for an opportunity to fulfill desires they keep buried under the fabric of business suits.

My phone vibrates with a message from one of these distasteful clients. He has a fetish for his daughter, which fascinates me. How does he find such attraction for the very being he created from his own loins?

Him: Hannah, can't wait to meet you again. I brought my daughter's clothes with me.

Me: She's definitely an adult?

Him: Yes, she's 25. She looks a lot like you, actually.

Me: Okay, it's going to be twice as much if you want me to dress like her this time.

Him: Anything you want. Meet me at the Bawdy Way Motel, outside of town, room 128.

I PULL INTO THE PARKING LOT. BAWDY WAY MOTEL flashes on a sign above me.

Bawdy—a nice, old-timey way of finding the humor in sex.

The building is whitish, with blue trim around the doors and windows. The paint looks fresh but is somehow still peeling in places. I park in front of room 128, which sits at the very end of the row. It seems to be the only room facing west. There's a wilted potted plant by the doormat and one sad plastic chair in which to sit and enjoy the view. I scoff. There's nothing worthwhile to look at here.

The 1 in the door number is tilted and missing one of its screws. I knock, but there's no answer. I grab the knob and turn it. It's unlocked, so I cautiously push the door open. I never know what I'm walking into with clients. Dressed in formal attire? Nothing but their birthday suit with a condom on their dick?

"Hello?" I call into the dark room as I try to find the light switch.

The door clicks shut behind me, and I'm surrounded by inky shadows. Not even the curtains over the windows let in a sliver of light. I turn for the door, my heart in my throat. Today is not the day I die by the hands of a man. With a shaking grip, I snatch open the door. Unfamiliarity greets me.

I expect to run for my car so I can get out of whatever nightmare I'm having right now, but the door opens into a hallway. The parking lot is gone. Oil lamps dot the hallway walls, casting a pale orange glow.

I turn back toward the room and gasp at the sight. The place looks clean, but it's so *old*. There's no electricity.

Candle sticks illuminate the corners of the room. Oil lamps stand on the dresser and bedside table. The flames flicker and leave a black rim of ash on the glass. The bed has a tall wooden headboard that almost goes to the ceiling. Its old wood contains beautiful carvings. The walls are covered in damask wallpaper with intricate patterns repeating throughout. I recognize that pattern because my grandmother loved all things wallpaper. Detailed paintings on the walls depict women in various stages of undress. I can almost feel the silk cloth draped over one woman's breasts. A faded rug with a floral design covers the planked floors. Across from the bed, a wooden chair waits beside a full-length mirror. Next to the chair is an old metal vase-like bucket.

I peek into the slightly agape drawer in the wooden dresser and find dresses folded inside. I've been holding my breath, and I inhale deeply, feeling as if my ribs are constricted. Looking down, I realize I'm not wearing the dress I came in here with.

Oh my god, there's so much fabric. I feel like I'm wearing a ball gown! And what is this?

I drag my hand down the taut fabric of the corset. When I look in the mirror, my chest is nearly up to my chin. I reach for nothingness, the strap of my purse gone from my shoulder. Even though I no longer have pockets, I still check for my phone. All my stuff is gone.

I ball up the fabric of the dress and lift it. Underneath, I'm wearing lightweight, fluffy shorts. There's a slit between the legs, and I definitely don't have panties on. Stockings stop at the pale skin of my thighs, and a garter wraps around my right leg. Delicate black lace adorns the top of the dress, and the sleeves drop down my shoulders. I release the skirt, and it falls back into place.

"What the fuck?" I try to sit down on the bed, but the corset makes it difficult. *How do you get this thing off?* I try to unfasten the front, but it's too tight.

The floorboards creak under my weight as I walk to the door. Confused, I head toward the muffled sounds and flickering lights at the end of the hall. The walls are made of old concrete, with wood paneling on the lower third, and there are paintings of horses and advertisements all along them.

I reach a railing and look over it. There are women dressed like me, sitting on the laps of men. They laugh and bat their eyes; I know that familiar look. The men drink from glass mugs and shot glasses. There's a man in a hat, playing a whimsical tune on the piano in the corner. His hands race along the keys.

The smells of must, sweat, and cigarettes assault my

nose. I creep down the stairs and past an old card table where several men have laid down cash on their hands of poker. They turn to look at me and tip their hats as I pass. My lips are tight as I fake a smile.

The saloon area has fancier floral wallpaper. The couches and lounge chairs here look out of place among the tables. Abandoned cigarettes lie in ashtrays as smoke rises from their discarded bodies. I walk past the large horseshoe-shaped bar, and the crowd becomes faceless. I'm lost in a sea of hats. Some have rounded tops, and there are even a few top hats.

I step outside. The wind sends dirt sailing because there are no paved roads. I shield my eyes from the sun as I take in the scenery. There's no parking lot and there are no cars. There are hardly even buildings here. A pair of hitched horses kick up more sand as they pull a covered wagon past me.

"This has to be some type of old-timey town reenactment. It must be for entertainment purposes. I mean, you see these things all the time." I try to reason with myself out loud, though I know it's irrational. What else can I do? This is *not* rational.

I look at the men skinning deer on my left. The woman to my right tries to palm off live chickens to any willing buyer. She has a look of desperation, as if food for her family depends on selling those chickens.

These people are quite good actors.

I walk back inside the saloon, which is dimly lit for the middle of the day. Candles flicker on the walls, and each table has its own oil lamp.

When in Rome? I think to myself as I head toward the bar.

The bartender is an older gentleman, with gray hairs sticking out from under an aged derby hat. He speaks with a gruff voice, without letting go of the hand-rolled cigarette in his mouth. "What can I get you?"

"Anything you have," I say with a hint of desperation.

He shrugs, pulls out a glass mug, and fills it with a gold-colored liquid. I expect a cold, thirst-quenching drink, but my lips meet with a room temperature, acrid tasting liquid.

"Can I have some ice?"

He turns to me, places the bottle down, and laughs. "Ice? Yeah . . . no, sweetheart. We can keep the liquor from being piss warm by wetting the gunny sacks in the basement and storing them in there, but we don't have any ice here in the desert." He shakes his head and grabs a wet rag to wipe the counter.

I turn away from him and take a sip of my drink. I can get past the warmth of the liquid, but I cannot get over the taste, scrunching my nose as I set the glass down on the bar. "Out of curiosity, what day is it?"

He looks at me with a raised eyebrow. He tilts his head and stops wiping the counter with the cloth. "It's the ninth of August, ma'am."

"But what year?" I look him in the eyes, my lips taut with frustration.

"Are you unwell, li'l lady? It's 1885."

1885?

A short woman enters the saloon, drawing my attention. Curled white hair frames her face, and her presence demands attention. She's the only one I see with jewelry made of fancy gemstones. She wears a lace gown, its fabric flaring out at the top. It envelops her neck and makes it look longer. She keeps a watchful eye over the women in the room, and soon her gaze falls on me.

I divert my attention, staring down at my glass and holding my breath. I hope she hasn't noticed me, but I can feel her presence approach my back. I turn around. Her head measures up to just above my chest, but her stare reaches into my soul with ferocity.

"Hello, I'm Madam Louise. Who are you?" she says with an excited lilt to her voice. Her eyes light up as if I'm a well-wrapped present on Christmas morning.

"I . . . I'm Hannah." My voice is small and is made even smaller when competing with the sounds in the bar.

"Okay, Hannah, why haven't I seen you before?" She reaches up and touches my hair, twisting the strands around her fingers. Her over-blushed cheeks are in sharp contrast with her painted white face.

"I'm new here." I speak with caution because I'm not sure where "here" even is.

"Where'd you come from? You have an accent," she says with a sultry expression. I stare at the creases in her lips as they move.

I take another disgusting sip of my drink. "I'm from New York."

"How'd a New York girl get all the way out here?" She places a hand on my arm, and I curl my lip at her touch, pulling away from her.

"A plane."

"Plane?" She raises her eyebrows but is unwilling to break her flirtation—not of a sexual nature, but a financial one. "You're a funny one. Why don't you come with me and meet some of my girls?"

A chair scrapes against the hardwood floors, and a man leaps from the poker table and tosses the wooden chair to the floor.

"Fucking cheater!" he says as he tosses more money on the table and leaves the saloon with heavy footsteps.

I turn my attention back to Louise and, with hesitation, I nod. What else can I do?

She takes my hand and guides me back upstairs toward an

open area to the left. There's a nice carpet, more paintings on the walls, and various furs draped over the furnishings. Several girls sit in the chairs dotting the room. Most are drunk and laughing loudly. Two of them have their corsets off, with their chemises falling open, exposing their breasts. When they see us, they hush and stand. The girls with their chests exposed don't even try to cover up.

"Madam Louise!" one of the girls exclaims from the farthest side of the room. She's met with a roaring hush from the girls around her.

"Girls, this is Hannah. I'm hoping to make her one of my own," she says with an unwavering confidence.

Your own? Not a chance. I belong to no one. I keep myself from rolling my eyes.

An older woman with dark hair brushes past me and scoffs as if she's seen this before. Another girl sits in her newly vacant seat.

"Ivy!" the madam calls to the dark-haired woman, but she ignores Louise and continues down the hall.

I look over at a woman standing just beneath a candle in the corner. The flame dances and flickers, offering me glimpses of her. She has porcelain skin that looks natural, unlike the madam's. Her lips are full and slightly spread. A mole rests above the left side of her mouth. Her eyes are light, but I can't tell the exact color under the glow of the candle. Her gaze is intense, but her expression is unreadable. Light blond hair is pulled loosely behind her head, with the rest draping over her shoulder. Her breasts are full—pulled together and upward by her corset. She's stunning and captivating, and I feel an aching in my gut to talk to her.

"Hannah," the madame says, "if you're willing to join us here, it's fifteen dollars a week for room and board. On top of that, the house gets twenty-five percent of your earnings."

The house? I can tell this place is a brothel, but I went into the escort business as an independent in order to avoid such overhead costs. I don't plan on paying any now.

I put my hands up and shake my head. "Oh no, I'm not staying. I'm just trying to figure out how to get back home."

Madam Louise draws in a quick breath, clearly disappointed. She motions me away as if shooing off a bothersome dog. The sounds of a commotion reach us from below, and with a quick suck of her teeth, she floats down the stairs in a hurry.

I walk over to the blonde, and she eyes me up and down. "You guys really get into character here," I say.

"We all have a part to play." She offers a sad smile and clears her throat. "But not everyone is cut out to play the role of a Bawdy girl."

I'm not sure if she means that as an insult or a warning.

"How do I get out of here?" I ask.

"You don't," says a slim red-haired woman. "It's easier to accept your lot in life."

"I don't think you understand," I begin, but she cuts me off.

"No, you aren't understanding. You're too mouthy to be a housewife, so you're better suited to putting your mouth to good use elsewhere, like moaning when a man climbs on top of you. You're no better than us, so stop acting like you are."

"Don't mind her," the blonde says. "I'm Belle, by the way." She offers me her hand.

"Hannah," I mumble as I take her dainty fingers in mine. Her skin is as soft as it looks. "I really do need to get out of here."

"Me too," she says, "but I never seem to be able to save enough to pay for passage to the next town. Not that it would matter. Sarah was right about that much. Some of us are better suited for lifting our skirts. Speaking of which, I need to get back to it if I want to make board this week." She stands to leave, and I follow her back downstairs. Instead of lingering in the saloon, I head outside.

The wooden porch creaks beneath my feet. A man dismounts his horse in front of me, and the animal snorts as the man hitches it to the post outside the building. He nearly knocks me over on his way into the saloon, as if his line of vision is clouded by the thoughts of liquor, women, or maybe a little of both.

I start down the sandy road, passing a few shops underneath fabric tents. I walk past wood and tools scattered where the bones of a building will lie. It looks as if they're constructing a church. I interrupt a man hammering a board into place.

"How do you get out of here?" I ask as I brush my hair out of my face, the wind whipping it from my fingers.

He stops working and looks up at me, wiping his brow with a cloth from the pocket of his vest. His collared shirt—white at some point—is stained with dirt and sweat. "Well, the only way out of here is by hoof or carriage."

"I mean, how do I *really* get out of here?" My voice is laced with frustration.

He looks at me with his eyebrows pulled together. "You can try walking, but the wolves or the savages will surely get to you by nightfall."

My brow furrows. "Savages?"

"You know, the indians." He picks up his hammer again and turns away, avoiding my gaze.

I sigh. I'm getting nowhere with the actors here, and I'll need somewhere to stay. Shielding my eyes from the sun, I look around at the other buildings. One has the word Hotel crudely painted above the doorway. I head toward it, climb the steps, and open the door. A bell chimes overhead, and a man pokes his head out of a backroom. He waits for me to speak. The customer service isn't all that great here.

"I'm looking for a room."

"It's three dollars a night," he says without taking a step out of his office. I feel for any pockets on the dress, a basic requirement for every dress I own. There are none, and my stomach sinks. I have no money, nowhere to stay, and no one seems willing to break character to help me get home. "Sorry for wasting your time," I say as I walk back outside.

I go to the barber in the middle of town. His face is friendly and approachable, a mustache curled above his lip.

"Is there an ATM here?" I ask with desperation.

"I'm sorry?"

My frustration wells within me until I can feel it threatening to explode from my mouth. The disconnect is apparent. It's like we aren't even speaking the same language! I swallow back the venomous words lingering in the back of my throat and take a deep breath. "Money. Where could someone go if they needed money?"

"If that someone were a woman, well, she'd really only have two choices: be a housewife or whore." He says this without looking away from his client. He finally catches my gaze and looks down at me. "I'd probably say a whore." He scoffs before motioning me away.

I return to the man still hammering boards of wood.

"Is there some kind of manager I can speak to?" I ask him as I cross my arms.

He cocks one eyebrow at me.

I close my eyes for a moment and suck in my cheeks, inhaling a deep breath. "Is there someone in charge of this town?"

He nods with sudden understanding and points to the building with the word Sheriff painted above the door. My skin beads with sweat, and I wipe it from my forehead before heading toward the sheriff's building.

There's a raised wooden platform next to the sheriff's

office—gallows adjacent to the building. The rope swings freely as the wind picks up. I gasp, noticing it's set up like a stage for viewing such distasteful acts. Children come to these sorts of places. I can hardly imagine a parent allowing their child to witness such a thing, reenactment or not.

After gathering my remaining sanity, I walk into the dark building. The interior is illuminated by a singular oil lamp on the sheriff's desk. A man is leaning back in his chair with a hat over his eyes. I clear my throat, and he startles awake, dropping his hand instinctively to his hip. He stands and adjusts his vest under his jacket before reaching his hand out to me, exposing a revolver on his belt.

"Hello, miss. I'm Sheriff Lane McGill. How can I be of service?"

"Well, I'm trying to get home. I ended up in some Wild West reenactment, and no one will help me get out of here!" Frustration explodes from my mouth.

He raises both eyebrows at me and cocks his head. He doesn't speak for what feels like an eternity. "Re-en-what now? Might we have had a little too much to drink at the Bawdy Way, ma'am?"

"Are you kidding me? *No!* This is ridiculous." I rub my temples. "I'll be leaving a scathing review about this place when I get home."

"Review?" He shakes his head. "Why don't you head back to the Bawdy and come back when you can act like a respectable lady?"

I huff as I turn around and walk back outside. I have no choice but to return to the saloon.

My feet are hardly off the steps before pounding hoof-beats stop me in my tracks. A cloud of dust rises as a man on horseback stops in front of the Sheriff's building. Another man is hogtied behind the saddle. Blood stains the buckskin coat of the horse. The rider hops down and tips his hat toward me before reaching over, grabbing the lifeless man, and dropping him on the ground.

I gasp as my eyes fall on the chest wound. Blood spreads over the fabric of his light work shirt. I would think it was part of the act if his eyes weren't so fixed and distant. I've seen this look more times than I care to admit. The skin is mottled and rotting from the heat. The cloud of flies descending on the body seem to have an invested interest in the corpse. The stench is putrid, and I shield my nose with my hand.

The sheriff walks out, and the man hands him the folded-up poster, which he reads aloud.

"Wyatt Whaley, wanted dead or alive for robbery of stage-coaches." He looks over at the man on the ground. "Dead, I see. I have reward money inside."

They head into the building, and I reach down and touch the dead man's skin. It's not a mannequin, and it's not an act. I look around with a sickening realization that this isn't just a reenactment. Tears well in my eyes.

What the fuck am I going to do?

I continue toward the Bawdy, shaking my head and repeating the word *no* over and over. I walk past the chestnut horse still hitched outside and point at it. *No.* I keep repeating that word in my mind, as if it will calm the panic in my chest. I climb the steps into the saloon, the door slamming behind me. Everyone turns their attention to me, and a man steps toward me.

"Hard fucking no!" I yell so loudly that the pianist stops his tune.

All the eyes in the room stare at me, eyebrows raised.

"Are you okay?" the bartender calls to me while wiping out a glass with a rag.

My cheeks flush. I gather my composure because I can't show fear in front of men. I never show fear in front of them.

"Carry on." I gesture toward the room before looking around for the madam. I catch a glimpse of her and start pushing my way toward her.

She sees me and her smile tightens and turns downward.

"Louise . . . I mean, Madam, can I talk to you for a minute?"

"I don't really think there's anything to talk about, dear." She turns away from me, and I sidestep around her and back into her line of vision.

If I'm stuck here, I need a job. "Well, here's the thing. I would like to work here but only in the bar area. You need servers, right?"

"Servers?" She raises her eyebrows.

"You know, bring the men their drinks and stuff," I say.

She lifts her chin toward me, as if I'm unworthy of her attention. "My girls do both." The madam lifts her hand and begins to turn away.

"Hey, I'm not above flirting! I'm just not interested in taking on clients." I glance around at the saloon full of gruff looking men, not entirely sure I want to serve them drinks either.

"You aren't one of those women who prefers the company of another woman, are you?" The madam swivels her head and stares at me with squinted eyes.

"No, no, I just don't want to do that line of work right now. I don't belong here. I need to get home, so I'll need money while I figure out how to do that."

She thinks for a moment, cupping her chin with her hand for dramatic effect. "Fine. You still owe board, but you can keep any tips that you get," she says before hurrying off to take control of an ensuing bar fight.

"But wait, where will I be staying?"

She's already gone.

I glance around and spot the beautiful blond from

upstairs. She's leaning over the card table with her breasts in the face of a player. His arm is wrapped around her with his hand settled on her ass. He slides a bill over to her, and she folds it up and puts it down the front of her dress. When she stands, my gaze catches hers. Once I'm in front of her, I can see that her eyes are an icy blue.

"Can I talk to you upstairs?" I whisper.

She looks around for the madam before nodding and accompanying me to the lounge area. She sits down in a padded chair and crosses her legs under her dress. I don't sit because I don't even think I can with this corset on. She reaches behind me and loosens the laces. The pinching sides of the corset spread enough that I can take a deep breath for the first time.

"Your corset was too tight. You want to trim your features, not crush them." She smiles at me, and I shiver slightly at her touch on my waist.

"Thank you." I try to sit down, the edge of the corset stabbing the flesh beneath my breasts. I lean back to ease the pressure. "I'm going to be hanging around for a bit. Louise said I could work the saloon area while I'm here."

"Just the saloon?" Belle's voice is surprised.

"Yes, I told her I wasn't interested in taking on men."

She lifts her chin slightly at my words, almost as if I've offended her.

"No, not that there's anything wrong with that," I say. "I'm an escort, actually." I take a deep breath, and my breasts fall to a more natural position.

"Escort?" Belle's voice rises as her eyebrows furrow.

"Yeah, you know . . . lady of the night? Hooker? Whore?"

"Whore? Why do you seem proud to call yourself that?" She cocks her head.

"Because I'm good at my job, and where I'm from, we don't need anyone but ourselves to do this business. I refuse to pay anyone a part of my earnings when I'm the one getting fucked."

"But who protects you? Where do you live? How do you find men?"

"I protect myself, I live in an apartment, and I find them on the internet."

"Internet?" She stares at me blankly.

Oh, for fuck's sake. "Never mind. I just need to know where my room is."

My frustration unintentionally spills over onto Belle, hitting her like a tidal wave. She rises from her seat, exhales a drawn-out breath, and gestures down the hall.

"The room that's farthest down the hall is the only one that doesn't have a girl in it now. I guess you'd be sleeping there."

I look down the hall toward where she pointed, and it appears to be the same room I came out of at the start of this whole thing. I thank her and nearly sprint to the room, hoping that maybe this is the signal to end this nightmare. I hang on to what little irrational hope I have left that maybe once she points or tells me to go back to the room, there's some kind of trick door that lets me back into my time.

I turn the doorknob and let myself in, but there's no other door. Only this one. I walk in and close it behind me, counting to ten before opening it again. No parking lot and no car. I loosen the laces of the corset until I can unfasten the front clasps and let it fall to the floor. I lie down on the bed and take a deep breath.

What the fuck is happening?

Chapter Three

I wake up in the middle of the night. I don't remember falling asleep. All I know is that I really need to pee. There's an intense aching in my pelvis. I'm still wearing my dress, but I have no interest in putting on that corset again. I walk into the hall and hear the sounds of men talking.

Does anyone sleep in this town?

I walk past the lounge area where several girls are sprawled out and asleep in the chairs with liquor mugs next to them.

Who hasn't been there?

I ease down the stairs and see several men still drinking at the bar. They tip their hats as I walk past. I approach the bartender—a much younger gentleman this time.

"Where's the restroom?"

"What?" He tosses the rag over his shoulder and cocks his head.

"The toilet?"

He stares at me until he finally grasps what I'm asking,

even if I hadn't chosen the right words. "Oh, out back." He points to the back door of the saloon.

I step into the cooler night air and head toward the wooden outhouse. It's missing a roof. *I'm pretty sure these are supposed to have a roof.* The smell is terrible, like baked shit. The stench of urine—more liquor than piss—encases me like a hug I don't want. Vomit on the ground in front of the outhouse is the metaphorical cherry on top of the bodily fluids.

I open the rickety door and hold my breath. The moon and stars provide the only light as they shine through the open top. A wooden box with a hole crudely cut out of the center stands before me. *You've got to be kidding. I can't use this!* I step away from the outhouse and look at the little field behind it, deciding it looks more appealing than the actual bathroom.

I hover behind the outhouse and try to hike the skirt of my dress. So much fabric. I pull down the fluffy undergarment with one hand. Even though they have a slit in them, I don't trust myself to avoid saturating them by mistake. I squat with one hand holding my dress and one hand holding the undergarments away from me. I sigh with relief as I finally get to pee. *Desperate times call for desperate measures.*

I stumble back into the saloon, trying to pull my shorts back up and my dress back down. Madam Louise cuts in front of me.

"What are you doing? You look like a mess." Her voice is harsh.

I look out the door behind me and motion toward it. "I just went to the bathroom."

"I notice that the men here are getting their own drinks, which is interesting because I thought I hired someone to do just that."

"Sorry," I say as I try to smooth my hair a bit.

"Go upstairs and please fix yourself up before you come back down!" she hisses.

I hurry back up the stairs, the skirt of my dress swaying.

I walk back into my room and open the dresser drawers. There are a couple other dresses, chemises, and skirts, and a few more pairs of the fluffy underwear. I wiggle out of the dress, fold it, and place it on top of the dresser before pulling out a chemise and slipping it on. I pull out a skirt and lift it over my thighs. My hands slip down the fabric, and I tuck the chemise into it. I grab the discarded black corset from the floor and pull it around my waist, fastening the front and working on the laces in the back. I can get it tight enough that my breasts perk under the pressure but not as much as in the tight tops of the dresses. My fingers brush through my hair as I pull it into a loose ponytail.

I return downstairs and find more men in the saloon. *It's literally the middle of the night. Do they not have a last call here?*

When I walk up to the bar, the bartender points at the drinks and then toward a small group of men. I bring them over and hand them each a glass while being sure to brush against their arms with my chest. Once everyone has been served, I have a seat with the only other women awake.

The two of them are intoxicated but not drunk. Like me, they're dressed down a bit for the night. Loose chemise fabric hangs down the brunette's shoulders. Dark strands of hair fall from her hair clip and frame her round face. She's the oldest one I've seen here. Her large breasts look uncomfortable, even on her full-figured frame. She eyes me as I sit down.

"You're the new one here, right? The one that won't sleep with the men?" She laughs and leans over to whisper something into the ear of the other woman. "I'm Ivy, and this is Sarah," she says, pointing to herself and then at the redhead beside her. She coughs as she drags a cigarette back toward her lips, the smoke wafting between us.

I had met Sarah once already, when I was talking to Belle. She doesn't show recognition on her face, whether intentional or not.

Sarah is very petite, almost as if Ivy has sucked all the weight out of her for herself. Her cheekbones are high, and her thin lips make her look a bit unapproachable. Her breasts are small mounds on her chest. She doesn't speak or give me more than a wave. I guess her lips aren't the only unapproachable things about her.

"I'm Hannah," I whisper as I stare at the cigarette with yearning. I almost ask for one, but Ivy starts talking.

"So, Hannah, you don't want to bed any men, eh? You think you're better than us?" Ivy says with a shake of her head.

"Actually, there's nothing further from the truth." I'm tempted to tell her about my lifestyle but decide against it.

Ivy scoffs and stands up. She nearly knocks her chair over in her haste. She grabs Sarah's hand, and they head over to the bar where they begin flirting with the men. Their skirts are heavy and don't move with their hips, which they try to accentuate as they walk. The fabric is colorful against the white, brown, and black hues of the saloon.

So much wood and plain-colored clothing in here.

I look around for the madam before heading to a room just past the bar. A smoking parlor, I assume. Belle sits near the window, a long stick resting on her lap. Her breaths are even as she lifts the stick and holds one end over a candle sitting on the table beside her. She puts the other end in her mouth and breathes deeply. Her body relaxes into the chair as she exhales. The smoke tumbles from her full lips and dances around her.

I walk over and sit beside her, but she doesn't notice me at first.

"What're you doing?" I ask as I lean toward her, my head craning to look at the pipe.

"Opium," she says with a sigh as her pupils constrict.

"Can I try?" I ask, hanging on to the slimmest bit of hope that this is still somehow a fake place with fabricated people —that I might inhale substanceless smoke.

She finally looks at me, and despite being high, her eyes look sad. She hands me the pipe, and I mimic her, breathing deeply. The vapors are warm, and the taste is unique. Almost flowery. It's a pleasant flavor, not like cigarettes or cigars. The high crawls from my lungs and crashes into my brain.

I lie back in the chair. These are definitely real drugs. Just one more thing to hammer the point home: I'm stuck here, and I'm not going anywhere anytime soon.

"Are you okay, Belle?" I ask, trying to break the silence between us.

She turns her face toward me, and I can see a cut above her right eye. There's still some dried blood surrounding the angry-looking gash.

"What happened?" I lean over and touch her cheek, making her flinch.

"Oh, you know, just another drunk who thinks they can smack you around a little." She speaks as if this is a common occurrence here.

"Oh my god, Belle. Did he get thrown out?" I probably know the answer—we're allowed to be punching bags here.

"Lord, no. *He* didn't cause this. Madam did. I told the guy to leave once he slapped me. Louise doesn't care what happens to us as long as she gets paid. Throwing him out was dollar bills walking out that door to her." She blinks away the gloss in her eyes. "I just want to go to bed."

Belle gets up to walk away, and I follow after her. We

don't speak because there's nothing more to say. Such is this life.

We head upstairs, the skirts of our dresses dragging along the dusty steps. My body feels light and airy from the drugs, which is a welcomed feeling. We stop at her door, just across the hall from my room. She opens it and walks inside, turning back with a half-hearted smile.

"I'm sorry," she whispers as she looks down at the ground.

"I'll see you in the morning?"

She nods and closes the door. I'm left alone in the hall-way, but there's no such thing as being alone here. I hear moaning and wood clanking against the walls from two of the surrounding rooms. Ivy and Sarah, I'm sure.

I walk into my room, closing and opening the door a few times to see if I can escape this hell. It doesn't work. The sound of fucking is somehow amplified as I get near my bed. Apparently, Ivy's room is right next to mine. Her moans are loud and obnoxious—clearly theatrical. A man groans, and the rattling and moaning stop. The door opens and slams before heavy, uneven footsteps trail away down the carpeted hallway.

CHAPTER FOUR

A knock on my door wakes me up. I look around and realize I'm still in this nightmare. Panic rises into my throat and makes it hard to swallow. I take a deep breath and answer the door.

Belle stands in the hallway with a kettle in one hand and a basin in the other. She walks into the room and places the basin beside the bed.

"Good morning!" she says cheerfully. The blood on her face is gone, leaving a thin, raw line in its place. She pours the water from the kettle into the basin and steam rises. She pulls a flannel rag from the top of her dress and places it on the rim.

"What is this?" My jaw goes slack, and my lips spread. I couldn't look more mortified if I tried.

"It's how you clean yourself off. How'd you do it in New York?"

"We have showers. Or baths. Literally anything other than *this*." I groan.

She tilts her head and purses her lips. "We do have baths, but we only get those once a week. What's a shower?"

"It's hard to explain." I sigh. "So that's it? I have to take a sponge bath?"

She shrugs her shoulders. "What else would you do? Just dump the water out the window when you're done cleaning up. I'll see you later." She offers a tight smile before leaving me alone with this bucket of disappointment.

I look down at the basin. The water is murky, with some debris floating around in it. I pull down my shorts and remove the chemise, dropping them to the floor before sitting on the edge of the bed. I pick up the rag and examine it. It looks clean, at least. I dip it into the hot water, wring it out, and sigh before I start wiping my skin.

I clean my face first, then my armpits, and lastly, my nether bits. No matter what I do, I don't feel clean. *How do these women lay with men knowing this is all you can wash them off with?*

I open the window, dump out the water from the basin, and hang the rag up to dry. The wood creaks as I open the dresser and pull out a deep-green day dress with black vertical stripes. This dress is higher in the front than the other one, allowing for just a teasing glimpse of my cleavage once I put on my corset. I pull on black stockings and run my hands along the fabric of the dress to smooth it over my hips. My fingers loop around each other as I braid my hair to one side.

I walk into the hallway and head toward the lounge area. It's empty for once. Laughter and music drift to me, and I continue down the steps into the saloon.

The bartender slides over a plate of potatoes and tough looking beef. I thank him as he hands me a fork, and I pick at the food before taking a few bites. It's so bland, and the beef is as leathery as it looks. I feel bad for ever taking cheeseburgers and showers for granted.

I pass the plate back to the bartender, and he hands me

two glasses of beer, motioning over to two men at the poker table. I walk over with the beer and sway my hips as I approach the table. I *really* need to make some tips if I'm going to be able to pay the board here. I lean over to place the glasses down and graze my chest against their arms.

One of the men has blonde hair and a long, thin nose, almost like a beak. He tips his hat toward me and slides a coin my way. I pick it up to look at it. It's a silver dollar. I tuck it into the top of my dress.

The other gentleman is much younger and has dark brown hair parted to the side. It looks wet—maybe oiled. His mustache is thick and curls upward but doesn't interfere with his lips. His brown pants go well with his brown jacket and black vest over a white collared shirt. His hat balances on his knee. He lifts it and puts it on his head so he can tip it toward me, which almost makes a smile creep across my face. He fumbles a bit, nearly spilling his drink. His eyes are locked on me as his lips curve into a sweet smile.

"I don't think I've seen you here before, have I?" he asks. The expression on his face is inviting.

I stare at him too long before I clear my throat and respond to his question. "No, I'm new here." I shift my weight onto my other leg, popping out my hip.

He notices.

"Ah, well, I'm Weston Willebrand." He tilts his head toward me, a half-smile on his face.

"I'm Hannah Moore." I reach out my hand, and he holds it for much too long. My cheeks flush, and I find myself noting his features in my mind, which is something I never do. Men are faceless.

The other man—The Beak—stands up, pulls me over to him, and sits me on his lap. His hand rests on my thigh before his fingers crawl higher. I try to stand, but he digs his nails into my flesh.

"Sir, I only bring drinks," I tell him firmly as I try to stand again.

"None of you only bring drinks." He laughs.

"Well, I do!"

Weston grabs The Beak's arm and pulls it away from me. He puts his hand on his hip, exposing the pistol on his belt. I find my feet and take a few steps back.

"She said she only brings drinks! Leave it alone," he says with a booming voice as his soft expression hardens.

Beak scoffs and lifts his beer as he gets up, leaning into me and speaking with disgust and a hint of alcohol. "I'll see you soon, ma'am." He tips his hat at Weston and leaves.

Weston motions for me to sit next to him. I happily oblige, taking a seat beside him. He takes a sip of his drink as his hand drops to rest on my arm.

"I'm sorry about that. There's not a lot of women here, it being a mining town and all. Some of us just get a bit too enamored when it comes to a beautiful woman." He smiles at me with his perfect mouth. His deep brown eyes remain locked on mine. "Have you ever played poker?"

"No, sir," I tell him as I watch his fingers toy with the old-fashioned playing cards.

Wes stacks his cards and puts them back in the pile. He slips his coins and bills back into his pocket.

"Well, I can't stay here and talk," I tell him when I spot the madam crossing the room. "I have to go back to work."

"What if I pay you to stay here and talk with me instead?" He stops my ascent before reaching back into his pocket. He pulls out a silver dollar and passes it toward me.

I look around for the madam before I pick it up and place it down the front of my dress. "I guess that would be okay." I sit down and arch my back slightly. "Tell me about yourself, Weston."

He puts his hand up to his mouth and plays with his

mustache. "Let's see. I'm a fourth-generation rancher. Cattle. I own the farm up on the hill, just outside of town."

"Married?" I ask, secretly hoping he'll say no.

"No . . . well, I *was* married. I lost my wife to fever two summers ago. She was with child, so I lost just about everything I stayed around this town for." He looks down at the table and shuffles the cards between his hands.

"Why haven't you left?"

"I guess it's cause of how much work my family put into that godforsaken farm. I can't bring myself to sell the cattle. Many go generations back." He passes another coin to me. "What about you? Where're you from?"

"I'm from New York. Came to Arizona for school."

"School? Aren't you a bit too old for school?" He flashes a toothy smile.

"I'm in College," I correct him, a grin creeping onto my face. A flush of heat rises to my cheeks.

"College?" He cocks his head at me, and his brow furrows.

"It's where you go to get educated. You learn all kinds of different subjects that help you with a career."

He sits back and twists his mustache. "Educated? Most people can't even read here." He smiles.

"Are you one of them?"

"I can read enough." He laughs, places his hat on the table, and brushes his hand through his hair before slipping another coin toward me.

I catch a glimpse of the madam and leap into Weston's lap, mouthing the word "sorry." He doesn't seem to mind. He wraps an arm around my waist and looks back toward her.

"I'm not getting you in trouble, am I?" he asks as he looks at me. His scent wafts into my nose—a rugged aroma, like dirt and soap.

"I don't know. I don't understand the rules of this place." My shoulders fall forward, and I sigh.

"The Bawdy?" he asks.

"Yes, but also everything else in this town. You guys bathe in buckets and shit in boxes!" I talk too quickly as I try to express the insanity of this place.

He laughs and pulls me closer. I can feel his excitement underneath me. The madam walks over and rubs a cold hand on the back of my neck, making me jump.

"Is she attending to your needs properly?" Her voice is sultry and laced with flirtation.

"Why yes, she's doing a fine job." Wes brushes some of my hair behind my ear, sending shivers reverberating through my spine.

She nods and walks away to check on the other girls.

I relax into him. "Oh god, that was close."

He smiles, slips a coin into the front of my dress, and looks up at me with eyes that reach into my heart. I don't know if he'll like what he sees there.

"I best be getting along now," he says. "It was a pleasure speaking with you, ma'am." He grabs his hat, places it on his head, and tips it as he leaves.

I walk up the stairs to put my coins in my room. In the lounge area, one of the other girls is on her back with her dress hiked up just enough to let a man clumsily fuck her. His pants are at his ankles, and his thrusts are quick but shallow. She isn't moaning or even pretending to enjoy it.

That's not good customer service. This is rule number one in the whore handbook.

I go to my room and lift the thin mattress. The coins rattle as I fish them out from the front of my dress and put them under the bed. I won't be able to afford board if I can't find other willing tippers. With a groan, I look around the room.

I touch the wall by the door, pressing my head against the cool wallpaper. It's so easy to imagine my car behind this wall. Somewhere . . . some place that isn't here. I open the door, praying to no one that I'll see the parking lot, the walkway, and my vehicle waiting for me. The only thing I'm faced with is the reality of the peeling damask wallpaper curling from the thick mixture of unfiltered cigarettes and body odor.

With no other choice, I head back downstairs to try to serve more customers. The bartender slides another glass of beer toward me, and it splashes on my dress.

Damn it.

I carry it to a patron who, despite my flirting, tips me with only a "thank you." I go back to the bar and pour out shots of whiskey for another group of men. They lift their heads, throw back their shots, and slam the empty glasses down on the counter. They turn to each other and start talking again. I didn't even get a thank you that time. A silver dollar does find its way into the front of my dress from a man who grabs my ass after I hand him his drink.

We are clearly only worth one thing to the men here.

CHAPTER FIVE

Madam Louise calls us into the lounge area with a shrill and excited voice. She flutters to each woman like a bee visiting every flower for a taste of pollen, reaching her hand out as coins and bills are dumped into her waiting grasp. She counts it out before depositing all of it into her bag. Belle seems to have made the most of anyone, and to know she takes on so many men both excites and sickens me.

The madam finally gets to me, and I drop eleven coins into her hand. She counts them slowly and deliberately. "Oh, Hannah, I see you didn't make enough to cover board." Her voice is condescending, as if she knew I wouldn't be able to make enough serving drinks—almost as if it had been her plan all along. "You'll owe me twice the board next week. Let me know if you change your mind about working the men."

"But . . ." I begin, my lip trembling.

"But nothing. These are the rules if you want to stay, little firefly."

Fireflies. They use bioluminescence to attract mates—or prey. Which one do I attract?

She pours the coins into her bag and puts a firm hand on my shoulder, squeezing hard and waiting for me to nod in agreement before she leaves. I try to remind myself that I'm unwilling to sleep with men for money here. The decision of who I lie with has and always will be my own. I'll sell my soul to the devil but not to some madam.

But I know I can't make double the board next week. Maybe I should take on just *one* client? It's not like I haven't done worse, and at least it will still be on my terms.

I follow Louise down the hallway and tap her shoulder.

She spins on her heels and feigns surprise when she sees me. "How can I help you, dear?"

"How much would I get for sleeping with one of the men?" I ask, my posture rigid.

She tightens her lips and touches my cheek with the back of her hand. "You, my dear, would get three dollars a lay. I would take the fourth."

My stomach twists. Four dollars? To fuck? I understand the currency conversion is different in this time period, but four dollars? That can't be all our bodies are worth here. It's almost comical, but I need the money.

"I have a proposition for you. If I take on one man, and you keep all the earnings, will you accept the board this week as paid in full?"

She thinks for a moment, hopeful she can pull me into this lifestyle after all. She nods after a moment of apprehension. "Ok, but it has to be by tonight."

She challenges me, probably hoping I won't be able to make it happen, but she doesn't know the truth about me. She's unaware that I *do* know my way around a belt buckle.

I loosen the strings at the top of my chemise, and the fabric spreads open to expose more of my cleavage. My shirt is tucked into a long, casual skirt because my two dresses are in the process of drying after being washed in a freaking bucket. I head down into the saloon and survey the room, knowing what kind of man I would want to lie with—someone with kind eyes and a soft demeanor. These are the men who typically appreciate sex with me, not ones who think they're owed it.

I set my sights on a tall, middle-aged man in a three-piece suit. The page of his newspaper rustles as he turns it while sipping on a glass of beer. He neither chugs his drink nor rushes to turn the page. I walk over and sit in the chair next to him.

"Can I get you another drink?" I ask.

He looks up from the newspaper with kind, stone-gray eyes behind gold-rimmed glasses. Just the eyes I had hoped for.

"Oh no, m'dear, thank you."

I nod and think for a moment. "Can I get you anything else?" I whisper as I put my hand over his arm and rub it softly.

His gaze drops away from me. "Nope, I think I'm all set," he says without looking up at me.

"Oh, ok. I was really hoping I could have my first time tonight." *Technically, I am a virgin in whatever fucking realm this is.*

This grabs his attention. He closes the newspaper and uncrosses his legs before pulling his glasses off and staring at me. "How much?" he asks.

I think for a moment. His suit urges me to inflate the price. "Twelve?" I smile at him.

"A little steep, but you seem worth it. Where's your room?"

I grab his arm and lead him upstairs. We pass the lounge on the left, which is thankfully vacant. I'm hoping for discretion. I look down and notice he has a slight limp.

"It's an old injury from when I worked in the mine."

"You don't work there anymore?"

"No, I own my own business now. I'm in . . . sales."

I don't know what the pause is about, and I'm not sure what type of illicit job would have to be cloaked with a fallacy here.

I close the door behind us once we reach my room. As I turn around, he puts a hand on my cheek and smiles.

"I'm Jedediah."

"Nice to meet you. I'm Hannah," I say.

Without hesitation, he leans in and kisses my neck. His hands wrap around my waist, sliding down my dress and stopping to rest at my ass. His kisses grow hungrier, and his hands grasp harder until he pulls away from me, breathless.

"I need to be the one lying down, m'dear. My leg just doesn't hold out like it used to." His steps are heavy as he walks toward my bed. He unbuttons his slacks and lies on his back. The fabric of his fly spreads open and exposes him.

I walk over to the bed and lift my skirt up to my hips. I straddle his waist and can feel how hard he is under me. The fabric envelopes our waists as I drop my skirt. I know why these shorts have a slit down the middle now. *Easy access.*

I reach down and help him find the warmth between my legs. Before I can pull my hand away, he's inside me. I lift and drop my hips rhythmically against his. His hands graze my waist as he reaches up and pulls the strings of my chemise, allowing the fabric to fall open further, exposing my breasts. He traces my nipples with his fingertips before grabbing the flesh of them. My moans fall over his as he grinds his hips into mine. I drop my head back, and his hands fall from my breasts, grasping my waist as I lean back. He thrusts beneath me, and I can feel the heat in my belly. It grows hotter until it burns, and I come.

What's better than a job where you get paid in cash *and* orgasms? *God, I miss my old life. Not this literal old life.*

He thrusts into me until he finishes, groaning into the

silence around us as he drops his hands to his sides. These men are so willing to fill you with their seed without a thought about the repercussions. My mind wanders, and I *really* hope my implant crossed over with me. I rub the area of my arm where it was injected under my skin.

He stands and buttons his pants before reaching into his pocket and pulling out some coins and bills. He counts it out and places it on the dresser. "Thank you, Hannah. It was a pleasure." He brushes my hair out of my face and kisses my cheek.

Jedediah is a unicorn client. I'm drawn to gentle men like the tide toward the moon, but it's not who I typically wind up in bed with. Men like *that* don't often want or need a woman like *me*.

The door shuts behind me as I finish tying the front of my chemise. I pick up the coins and dollars from the dresser and put four coins down the front of my shirt. The rest goes under the mattress as insurance for next week. The madam would break my legs if she found out, and I shiver at the thought of what the consequences would be for stealing from the house. Is it really stealing, though? I had to lie down to earn the money. I hardly own my body here; it's merely on loan from the madam.

I walk into the hall and head past the lounge. The madam sits in one of the chairs with her legs up on a bench. She's filing her nails. I approach her, pull out the four coins, and set them on the arm of the chair.

"That was quick," she says. "I knew you had it in you."

"Don't expect it again," I snap back.

"I won't . . . as long as you can pay your board next time. This isn't a charity." She sucks in a deep breath and puts her hand up to dismiss me.

I head back toward my room but hover outside Belle's door. I knock, and her voice welcomes me inside. A beautiful ocean-blue dress and white corset hug her frame. A mound of coins and bills rests on the table beside her. She holds a cigarette between her long fingers. She places it between her lips and breathes deeply before flicking the ash out the window.

"I heard you with a client." She looks up at me and brings the cigarette back to her lips, inhaling the smoke as if trying to rid her lungs of oxygen.

"I had to. I didn't have enough this week."

"I saw," she says with sadness in her eyes.

I reach over and spread her money across the table. *There's at least forty dollars here. How?* "Belle, how do you take on so many clients in a day?"

She looks at me, and the corners of her lips draw up in a smile. "You have to learn the thigh trick."

"The thigh trick?" This excites me. Maybe it's something I can use in my own time . . . if I can ever get back there.

"With the really drunk ones, you just put their cock between your thighs. They don't know you from a hole in the wall at that point. They can't tell the difference."

I sit beside her and envision drunk and clumsy men making love to the soft flesh of her legs. "That's really helpful, actually. Do you mind if I have a drag?"

She hands me the cigarette, and I bring it to my lips, drawing in the smoke and letting it fill my lungs. There are definitely no filters in these—just straight tobacco—and the full strength sends me into a coughing fit. Belle leans back against me, letting her body melt into mine. Her hair is in a braided bun at the nape of her neck. Loose strands fall down her cheeks, and I brush them behind her ears.

She's beautiful, and I'd be lying if I said the heat of her body didn't ignite something inside me. I cross my legs to tame my desire. I can understand why the men seem to prefer her. I've never been with a woman but lying with Belle makes me consider it. What would it feel like to have her mouth between my legs?

"Do you girls ever . . . you know . . . fool around with each other?" I ask. My question is full of hope and hesitation. My intention isn't to offend her, but her silence makes me question if I may have. "I shouldn't have—"

"We aren't supposed to," she interrupts, sitting up to face me as we talk. "It's considered immoral for a woman to lay with another woman." She looks around the room cautiously before rolling her eyes. "But let me tell you, none of these men seem to know their way around my business better than another woman does." She laughs and covers her mouth as if she's just told me a devilish secret.

My heart breaks for her. If she lived in my time, she'd be free to explore her desires instead of hiding them behind closed doors.

"Besides," she continues, "the women don't take from you. They don't beat you into submission and treat you like a used-up piece of equipment." The smile falls from her face.

I pull her into me again. "Oh, Belle. You're not used up." Even if she feels it on the inside, she doesn't look like it on the outside. Her skin is so beautiful and untarnished. Even the slight curve of her nose is perfection. She's like a rose blooming in the desert—she can't help where she's been planted. I'm a wilted carnation tossed onto the sand to rot. "You're the only one I can call a friend here. Those other girls are insufferable."

"Tell me about it. You learn to ignore them, though. Just steer clear of Ivy and Sarah, and you'll be fine." She pats my thigh, her slender fingers lingering. "We shouldn't be snuggled up like this. If Madam Louise catches us, she's liable to cast us out."

"Cast us out? Is it really that serious?" I find it hard to believe.

"It would be suicide, Hannah. There's nothing else out there for women like us. Without a marital bed to fall into, we'd have nowhere to live. And no one wants to wed a whore." She bites at her bottom lip and looks into the distance for a moment, as if remembering something painful. The look vanishes off her face, and she forces a smile, but I don't miss the misty look to her eyes. "Well, you'd best go before the madam gets suspicious. Thanks for considering me a friend." She kisses my cheek and I leave.

The sweet scent of her perfume lingers long after I'm back in my room, as does the ache between my thighs.

CHAPTER SIX

I spot Weston across the saloon. He's wearing brown pants and a black collared shirt under a leather jacket. His hat is different and darker than the one he had when I saw him last. I deliver two glasses of beer to a pair of patrons and accept a tip before I catch his attention.

He sees me, smiles, and tips his hat. "Hannah!"

"Hello, Weston. I wasn't sure if I'd see you again." The heat creeps to my cheeks and crawls across my chest.

"There's no other saloons in town." He laughs and hands me a silver dollar.

"You know, Weston, I can't keep taking money from you like this." I slip the coin in my dress and smile at him as he grabs my hand and leads me outside. The air is dry and stagnant, and the heat of the day causes a shimmer to rise off the sand.

"This is Concetta," he says, introducing me to a large black horse hitched outside the bar. Her mane and tail are as dark as her coat.

I touch her muzzle, and she nickers in response. Her hide

is warm, and I can't imagine wearing a black fur coat in this heat. Weston mounts Concetta and reaches a hand down to me. I look back toward the saloon.

I want to go with him—he's handsome, charming, and it would get me away from this awful place for a bit—but I fear the wrath of Madam Louise. I'm not even sure this sort of thing is allowed.

"I can't leave," I say as I look around for curious eyes.

"Sure you can. I'll pay you for your time," he says.

I shrug and grab his hand as he helps me onto the back of his horse. Sitting on horseback with a skirt is not easy or comfortable, and the hot leather saddle scalds the skin of my thighs. He pats the horse's neck as I wrap my arms around his waist, and he urges Concetta forward. Her hoofbeats create a soothing rhythm in the sand as we ride past the wooden sign welcoming people to the town of Sundown.

"Have you ever been on a horse before?" he asks, his body moving comfortably upon his mount.

I want to say yes, but my thighs and ass are saying no. "I rode a horse a few times when I was younger. Hardly a cowgirl, though."

"Well, hang on, ma'am." He taps Concetta's sides with his spurs, and she starts trotting.

I squeeze Weston harder to stop my breasts from bouncing out of my top. "Oh, I don't like this!" I yell to him as I bury my head against his back.

Weston laughs and urges her into a canter. The movement is much smoother, like a rocking horse. We follow a winding road. Cacti stretch out from the hot and sandy soil, each node exploding with sharp spines.

Concetta slows to a walk as we approach her home. I look past Weston's shoulder and see a small wooden house. Wooden fencing beside it holds a few more horses, and

Concetta whinnies at the sight of her herd. Weston dismounts and reaches a hand up to me, helping me slide down to the ground. My skirt catches on the saddle, exposing the pale skin of my thighs. I blush and unhook the fabric. He stares at me as he releases the girth and untacks Concetta, smiling as he wipes the dust off his hands and onto his pants.

"You're a natural!" he says with a smile.

He unties the rope holding the gate closed and drags it open, creating a line in the sand. He walks Concetta into the pen and slips off her bridle, allowing her to trot in and nuzzle a bay horse.

Weston grabs my hand and walks me into his house. A wire handle holds a teakettle over the fireplace. The wood is charred but flameless. Old wooden chairs surround a small table in the one-room home. A box sits next to it, filled with salted meat. On the other side of the room, a small dresser stands beside a full-sized bed covered with a fur blanket. Everything in here appears to be handmade. Every piece of furniture has the unique touch of a man and his blood, sweat, and tears.

Weston grabs the kettle and pours water into two tin mugs before handing one to me and taking a hearty drink. "So, I thought maybe you could help me with something." He smiles at me as he gestures toward a pile of clothes near the bed.

I look up at him curiously and take a sip of the water. It's piss warm but soothes my dry throat. "You're paying me to do chores for you?" *I'd almost rather take on men.*

"I'm paying you fairly for your time, Miss Moore. I think this is mutually beneficial. I need help, and if you're just going to work the bar, you need money. I swear I've washed them since Mary died. I just don't have the time lately. The cattle need to be driven and fed. The goats also need to be milked." He wipes the sweat from his brow and looks down at me, his gaze pleading. His rich brown eyes reach inside me, but I'm not the domestic type, and I'm not sure what about me implies that I am.

"Fine!" I say, rolling my eyes.

"Thank you! The bucket and washboard are just out here on the porch," he says.

I follow him out the door.

His eyes snap to the open gate of a round pen and a couple of cows running off toward the hills. "Well, shit." He runs over to close the gate. "The pump is just behind the house!" he shouts back to me, draping the rope over his shoulder. "I'll be right back! I promise!"

I nod to him and wave him off as he runs toward the horses and disappears around the corner. I pick up the bucket, and a little black block rattles inside of it. With my other hand, I grab the washboard and walk toward the back of the house. I place the bucket down and touch the handle of the water pump. It's a deep reddish-brown from rust. I try to crank it, but doesn't budge, so I stand behind it and use all my strength to pull it. When it finally loosens, I lose my balance and fall backward onto my ass. I scoff, stand, and wipe the dust from the back of my dress.

The water flows onto the sand, turning it a dark-brown color. I slide the bucket under the stream, and it fills with suds. *Oh, the black block is soap!* I fill it halfway and carry it back toward the house, dropping it onto the floor as soon as I get it inside. The water sloshes and spills over the rim. I wipe the sweat off my forehead with the skirt of my dress. I would almost prefer to make money on my back than to do labor like this, but Belle's words replay in my head.

"There's nothing else out there for us."

My face scrunches as I pick up the pile of clothes and set

it down next to the bucket. A knife slips from the pocket of a pair of pants. I slide it into my garter so I can give it back to Wes when he returns. I grab each item of clothing and dip it into the soapy mixture. The smell of dirt and sweat wafts toward my nose. I run the fabric along the washboard and hang it up to dry on the line that goes from a hook next to the door, across the porch, and loops around one of the railings. When I finish, I stand back and put my hands on my hips to admire my work.

Heavy hoofbeats approach the house. I may not know much about horses, but I can tell there's more than one. I shield my eyes from the sun and try to see who it could be.

"Weston?" I yell into the stale air, but I hear no response. Heavy footsteps startle me, and I turn around.

Two men stand at the end of the porch with their pistols drawn. The sun reflects off the metal of their firearms. They have on dingy undershirts and pants with rips and tears in them. Their long, dirty hair falls into their sand-covered faces.

I put my hands up as they walk closer to me, circling like a pair of vultures. They poke at my dress and lift it up before letting it fall back down, taunting me.

"Where's the man of the house?" one of the men says. "Shame to leave a beautiful girl like you by yourself." He rubs the barrel of his pistol on my cheek.

"He'll be back any moment," I say with feigned confidence, unwilling to show these men any weakness.

"Is that so?" He looks at his friend. "We came for cash, but I think we found something better, Roy. Don't you?"

Roy nods and starts unbuttoning his pants. I flinch as he lifts my dress and puts his filthy hands on my hips. I don't react the same way most women would to a man taking me against my will. I learned that pleading only gets them harder, and fighting them makes them hit you. To get out of it alive and with nothing but your dignity lost, you comply. Tears slip down my cheeks as he prods between my legs with a half-limp cock. The sound of hoofbeats gives me hope, and I try to yell for Weston.

Roy covers my mouth with a hand so dirty that his nails are black. Weston steps across the porch and into the two bandits' line of sight. The nameless one with the gun against my face yells something unintelligible to Roy. Weston's gun emits a *click* as he cocks it and continues walking toward us. His steps are sure, without a hint of hesitation in his stride. Roy panics and tries to pull up his pants.

Weston fires a shot through Roy's hat, and the bullet knocks it off his head and onto the ground. Roy reaches for it with wide eyes.

"The next one won't be in the hat." He cocks his pistol again and continues to step toward us.

They run off, nearly falling in their haste. Weston takes one step back, as if he were planning to give chase. I collapse to the porch, tears falling relentlessly, and he turns toward me. Yes, I react differently in the moment, but not once the threat is gone.

Weston holsters his pistol as he squats in front of me. "Hannah, I'm so sorry!"

I'm breathless and my chest heaves, making it difficult to speak. "Who were those people?"

"Road agents, if I had to guess," Wes says as he looks back toward the road.

"Road agents?"

"Thieves," he says with distaste.

"And rapists," I whisper under my breath.

He wraps his arms around me and lets me cry into his chest. His undershirt and jacket are covered in dust. He sits down next to me and looks into my eyes as he puts his hand over mine. "He didn't? Did he?"

"No. Not this time." I drop my gaze to the wood of the porch and concentrate on the cracks in the boards, trying to forget how many men have taken such an unwilling part of me in the past.

He interrupts my memories when he reaches over and touches my cheek with his hand. "I'm sorry, Hannah." His face is soft and saturated with guilt. "I couldn't even find a trace of the damn cows."

"I have to get back, Weston." I realize the irony of my words as soon as they leave my lips. I have to get back to my time, not just The Bawdy.

"At least let me fix you a bite to eat before you head back. I know what kind of food they serve at that place." He lets out a laugh. "I'll even pay you a little extra for your company?"

I can't say no, and it's not just the offer of more pay. His dark eyes make my stomach clench, and I wouldn't mind staring into them a little longer. I draw a deep breath and nod. A smile breaks across his face, and I follow him inside.

He sets to work in the simple kitchen, and the scent of salted meat soon fills the air. I'm not sure what to expect from a man who's lived on his own, but I'm surprised when he sets the metal plate before me. It's a far cry from the meal I had with Thomas not so long ago: dry cornbread with a slice of fatback and some stewed potatoes. Yum.

"Thanks," I say through a forced smile. "It looks . . . great." I don't want to hurt his feelings. He looks so pleased with himself. I shovel a forkful into my mouth and chew, fighting back the urge to chug the warm glass of water with each bite. "Mmm," I say with raised eyebrows.

He tucks into his food, not noticing my feigned enjoyment. I've gotten good at faking it over the years.

"You sure you're ok after what happened earlier?" He pushes his cleaned plate away. "If they hurt you in any way—"

"I'm ok, Wes. I've been through worse."

He clears his throat. "Who? Who else has put their hands on you?"

I can hear the protective nature in his voice. It's strong and husky, making me both nervous and attracted. "No one around here."

"Back in New York?"

"Um, yeah." I can't very well tell him it's more like one hundred and fifty years in the future. "It's not a big deal."

"It is a big deal. If anyone around here lays a hand on you, I want to know about it."

I don't know how to respond. I'm not used to having someone in my corner. I'm used to fighting the battle alone and licking my wounds later. "I appreciate the meal and everything you've done, but I really have to get back to The Bawdy. I'm sure Madam Louise will have my head after this."

He nods and stands up, reaching down and offering me his hand. He fishes through his pocket and withdraws several dollar bills and some silver dollars.

"For your time," he says as he gestures toward the cash.

It seems almost distasteful for me to take money after this, but I do need it. If I go home with nothing, I won't be able to pay board. I roll the coins into the bills and stuff the mass into my dress as we walk out the door.

Concetta is hitched by the house. He puts a leg in the stirrup and mounts her with ease before reaching his hand down and helping me up. I look down and shiver as I see the frenzied hoofprints left by the bandits. I reach my arms around Wes and hold myself against him. Concetta canters toward town, and we ride with silence between us. I'm drawn

57

into my own head, tormented by the memories the bandits triggered.

We reach the saloon, and Weston dismounts before helping me down to the ground. He fumbles with his hat in his hands. "I'd understand if you didn't want to come back to the farm. I'm sure it didn't create a great first impression. Actually, not even a good one."

"Oh, it was a terrible first impression." I smirk at him, and he looks down at his hands, his tan cheeks still managing to flush with a pink hue. "But I'd like to go back when you're willing to take me." I curse myself for such flirtation. Nothing good comes from men, especially lawless ones.

He looks up at me, smiles, and places his hat on his head, tipping it toward me before mounting Concetta. I wave and turn to go back into the saloon.

Ivy stands in the doorway, smoking a cigarette. She squints her eyes, and I can't tell if it's from the sun or suspicion.

She sucks her teeth. "Hm, you seem like you've been mighty busy."

It is, in fact, suspicion.

"At least I can get clients," I snap back. I'm not going to cow to her.

Her jaw drops. As I push past her, she kicks out her leg, tripping me and sending me sprawling across the floor. Two coins roll from my cleavage. I watch in horror as she covers them with her shoe and bends to retrieve them. My livelihood is crushed beneath her foot.

"Leave it," comes a voice from the staircase. It's Belle. She shuffles down the steps and stands in front of Ivy, challenging her with an icy stare.

With nostrils flaring, Ivy considers for a moment before pulling her foot away and stomping off. Belle picks up the coins and hands them to me. She offers me her soft hand and helps me to my feet, dusting off the front of my dress.

"Quite the entrance," she says with a smile.

"Thanks." I brush a stray piece of blond hair from her forehead and smile back.

We stifle a giggle and head upstairs.

CHAPTER SEVEN

I brush through Belle's hair with my fingertips before braiding it and wrapping the braid around the back of her head. It sits on her head like a crown. She turns to face me, and I guide the loose strands behind her ears. Her lips are close to mine, and her breath is warm on my chin. I cradle the back of her head and crane my neck to kiss her. She kisses me back.

Belle is safety. She's the only one I can open up to here.

When she pulls away from me, she's biting her lip. I lean into her and lay her down on the bed. My hand teases up her thigh and crawls beneath her green dress. She lets out a quiet moan against my mouth. Aside from a garter on her thigh, she isn't wearing anything under the folds of fabric. I play with her between her legs while kissing her. I lift the skirt toward her hips—*so much fabric*—and drop down on my knees, pulling her hips toward my face.

She sits up, her eyes wide. "What are you doing?"

"I'm going down on you?" I say with a soft pout of my lips and hunger for her on my tongue.

"We don't really put our mouths . . ." Her normally gentle

fingers grow firm on my wrists as she stops my wandering hands. The look of discomfort—the hardening of her features —squelches the excitement between my own legs. There's intense fear in her eyes, rounding them and making her lips quiver. She scoots backward and draws her knees to her chest.

I climb up beside her with a sigh, my fingers picking at the skirt of my dress. "I'm sorry, Belle. I got a bit carried away." I flash my eyes at her, but she doesn't look at me. After a few minutes of silence, I clear my throat, trying to come up with something to pull her from whatever memory she's locked in. "Can I ask you a question?"

Belle toys with her thin fingers before nodding.

"What do you remember the most about clients?" I ask.

"Well, I reckon it's their sounds. These noises of pleasure that just seem so pained to me. Like they're trying with all their might to hurt me and push all their frustration into me, but instead, it's just blowing out their mouths in grunts. What about you?"

"For me, it's their smells. I can drown out their sounds if I think hard enough, but my nose can't seem to ignore their scents. I remember this one client I can only describe by how he smelled—sour body odor and suffocating cologne trying to mask it. The moment I met him and got a look in his eyes, I knew I wanted to leave. The metallic sound of the lock as he closed the door sent goosebumps up and down my arms. My body reacted before I even knew what was coming."

"Oh, Hannah." Belle gasps as if she knows this story all too well.

"Do you want me to stop?" I ask, watching her eyes focus their intensity on me.

She shakes her head.

"This moment of realization set in, and I knew I was going to be raped, murdered, or maybe a little of both. I thought my mom would find my dead body in this sad hotel room, wearing the skimpiest dress I could afford at the time. There'd be no explaining away why I was there, but she'd still try."

"What happened next?" Belle asks, dropping her hands to her sides. She's drawn into the story of a time when my soul was still full of life and my heart was still capable of feelings.

It was the beginning of the end for me.

"Well, he raped me. It was weird because I felt like I was hovering over my body and watching it happen to someone else—someone with the same hair and glassy eyes. I can still feel the hollow pit in my stomach . . . the pain between my legs with every thrust. I remember the buckle of his belt rhythmically smacking against the table by the bed." I knock on the wooden table beside Belle's bed. "The more I flailed beneath him, clawing at the blanket like a scared animal, the faster that buckle hit the table."

What I can't put into words is how it felt as he climbed off me, taking such a big part of my innocence with him. From that position above my body, I could almost see this black smoke between us, swirling around before he sucked it into his mouth and down his throat. And there it would remain indefinitely.

After a few moments of silence, Belle finally spoke. "My first time was forced. My mama brought me here when I was fifteen. Sold me off to the madam once my daddy died. Guess she couldn't be bothered with me anymore. She never liked me much, anyway. She was always getting drunk and thinking I was running off to lay with the boys in town." She drew a deep breath. "I never even so much as lifted my skirt above my ankles around any boys. It didn't matter to her, though. She thought I was a whore, so she forced me to become one."

My eyes lock on to hers. "You were a virgin when you came to The Bawdy?"

"Oh yes. The madam threw me a party and let me drink as much as I wanted. There was music and dancing. I thought maybe this place would be okay, but then the bidding started."

"Bidding?"

"On me. My virginity. I was pure, and it excited Louise in ways only money can."

"Who won?"

"I had my first sexual experience beneath the rich, old owner of some fancy new railroad in town. He wasn't all that mean, but he kept saying how much he paid to have me whenever I told him no. His skin was really . . . I don't know. He felt like leather that got dried out in the sun. I just remember the sound of it as it slapped against me. He howled as he came. *Howled.*" She forces a grin as she lifts her chin and mimics the sound as quietly as she can. Her giggle is at an uncomfortable moment, but I can't help but laugh myself as I remember a man who said the Hail Mary prayer at the top of his lungs as he unloaded into the condom.

I embrace Belle and breathe in her scent.

There's an unexpected knock on the door, and I quickly scramble to my feet, tugging Belle up beside me just in time for the door to open. Madam Louise stands in the doorway. She looks at me, at Belle, and then back at me.

"What are you doing?" she asks as she squints her eyes in suspicion.

"I was just braiding Belle's hair." I turn Belle around to show the madam the new crown braid.

She reaches out her small, wrinkled hand and touches Belle's hair. She coos. "That is beautiful." Louise turns her attention back to me, and her lips purse. "We need to talk, Hannah." She looks at Belle. "In private."

I follow her toward my room, and she shuts the door behind me.

"What do we need to talk about?" I ask with genuine innocence. It could be about any number of things I've done or haven't done.

"Ivy told me something very interesting."

"About?" My voice is laced with annoyance. Of course Ivy went to the madam. When you're as old as Ivy, you don't keep your position by keeping your nose clean.

"It seems that instead of working the bar, which I hired you for, you went gallivanting around with some rancher."

I turn around, pull the board money out of my dresser drawer, and shove it in her face. "He paid me to do some work for him."

"Work *for* him or work *under* him?" She lifts her eyebrows.

My eyes squint at her. "It shouldn't matter what I do as long as you get paid."

"No one, and I mean no one from under this roof, will lie on their back without giving me my cut."

I lean over a bit to meet her at eye level. "I haven't fucked him, but regardless, you can either let me get paid my way, or you can lose out on that weekly board. I only bed the men that I choose. This place won't change who I am. I am my own madam!"

She slaps me. Her ring cuts my cheek, and when I reach up and touch the painful flesh, blood comes away on my fingers. Louise slams the door as she leaves.

I sit on the bed and work off my corset so I can breathe freely. My breasts can finally relax under the soft material of the chemise. I wipe nervous sweat from my forehead. I wasn't sure if her anger was going to be over Belle or Wes, but I'm glad it's the latter. I can handle myself regarding my peculiar outings with Wes. I can defend myself from that narc, Ivy.

Ivy. Even her name is poison, like the three leaves you should leave be. An opportunistic plant sitting in wait to cause an inconvenient and itchy rash.

I walk downstairs and enter the saloon, my eyes searching for Ivy. I see her step out the side door, so I follow her outside. She holds a cigarette between her short fingers and thin lips. I stand next to her and put my foot on the wall behind us. She eyes me.

"Can I have a smoke?" I ask, watching the stained tip of the paper leave her lips.

With a roll of her eyes, she hands me the cigarette.

I take a deep drag and hand the cigarette back to her, blowing the heavy smoke in her face. "I'm going to kindly ask you to mind your own fucking business, you old hag. If you think about telling Louise anything about me, please take a moment to think twice." I pull Weston's small knife from under my skirt. It flickers in the sun. "Am I understood?" A plastic smile creeps across my face, my teeth clenching in anger.

"You better watch yourself. It's real easy to get burned around here," she says as she takes a drag, the cherry glowing red. Ivy drops the cigarette onto the sandy ground between us. She looks at me with the same numbness to threats that I have. This job does that, regardless of where we are in time. She pushes past me and knocks her shoulder into mine, and I look around before I slip the knife back into my dress.

I need to remember to give this back to Weston, but as my fingers graze the handle of the blade, I wonder if I should keep it.

Chapter Eight

I take a walk, not quite ready to go back into the saloon. My steps kick up dust and the sun warms my skin in moments. The heat here is dry and suffocating. A large man in a white apron stands behind the table of a wooden stand, coolly slicing chunks of meat from a cow carcass. Blood drips from the hanging body and lands in a pool at his feet. He greets me with nothing more than a grunt. The word Butcher is crudely written on a banner in front of the booth.

I continue until I reach another booth where a well-dressed barber shaves the beard of another man. His hands work flawlessly with his blade, as if he's an artist. The sun catches on the metal and shoots a blinding glare toward me.

I finally stop at a building that says General Store above the doorway. A bell chimes over my head as I walk in. I stroll past a table of fruits and vegetables and pick up an apple, rubbing it against my dress before taking a bite. On a shelf nearby, canned foods have been stacked beside boxes of ammo. Fine china pieces are scattered throughout the store, with little price tags dangling from their edges. In the corner, alcohol bottles stand beside various medicine bottles. The one labeled Morphine catches my eye.

"You can just buy this over the counter here?" I ask myself with wide and curious eyes.

I look up at the advertisement above the medicine. It's for a cocaine teething medication. *Cocaine! For babies!* Another bottle's label reads Extractum Cannabis. Weed extract. *For how awful most of this place is, they sure know how to party.*

I pick up a small glass bottle of laudanum. *Like in the movies?* I shrug, walk up to the shopkeeper, and hand him the bottle. I avoid his gaze as if I'm buying something illegal. It's like when I buy Sudafed over the counter, and I can't help but wonder if they think I'm going to cook up a batch of meth later.

"It's not for me."

"Okay. Fifteen cents, please."

"Oh, and the apple."

"Twenty cents," he says as the tray of his cash register pops open.

I reach down the front of my shirt, pull out a silver dollar, and slide it to him across the wooden counter. He puts it in the register, hands me change, and pushes the bottle toward me, which I slide down the waistband of my skirt.

The bell chimes again as I step outside and turn to head back toward the saloon. I pass the butcher, whose apron is now covered with blood. He nods as he wipes his forehead with the back of his hand, leaving a streak of blood on his face.

I cross the road and see Beak standing in the saloon's doorway. My heart races, thumping against the front of my chest at the sight of him. My mouth goes dry as he smiles at me, exposing his chipped yellow teeth. He tips his hat toward me, and I decide to take the side door instead.

The patrons in the saloon absorb my body as I head

toward my room to place the bottle of laudanum in one of the dresser drawers. Beak stops my ascent on the bottom step.

"Can I have a drink?" he asks with a low, sultry voice.

My breath hitches in my throat, making my words shake. "What do you want?"

"Whiskey." He watches me as I head to the bar.

"A shot or glass?" the bartender asks, and I look back at Beak, trying to anticipate his choice.

"Uh, a glass." I carry the glass and hand it to Beak with the most unfriendly look I can muster.

"Are you still just serving drinks?" He tosses a coin at me, staring as he touches my upper arm and uses a finger to drop the fabric of my chemise over my shoulder.

"Yup."

He growls, reaches a dirt covered hand up to my face, and curls a finger against my cheek. I lean away from his touch, and he lets out a deep, ominous laugh.

I run upstairs and into the lounge area to try to catch my breath. You can't let men see you scared—especially not here. Our worth is grossly undervalued. We hold so much power, yet none at all. I guess nothing has changed when it comes to the women of the night.

Footsteps fall on the wooden planks behind me. Assuming it's one of the other girls, I don't turn around. Fingers wind into my hair, and my head is forced into the wall. I fall to the floor and try to put my hand up to my head instinctively. I twist my body so that I'm on my back.

Beak hovers over me. His body is large and overbearing in this position, even though he isn't a tall or heavy man. He grabs a fistful of my hair and drags me toward a bedroom. The wood scrapes against my knees as I crawl to keep up with him.

One of the other girls walks out of her room and looks at

us. I plead with her with my eyes, and she takes a quiet moment to assess the situation. She looks at me with no surprise or excitement. She displays no real emotion at all. It's almost as if she's seen this before—or has lived this before. She lifts her glass to her lips and steps over my legs to walk past me.

Beak chuckles to himself and tosses me into the room, closing the door behind him. *I should have screamed! Why didn't I scream? Curse me for always being such a stoic whore.*

"Stand up." His voice is deep and commanding as he watches me stumble to my feet. "Take your clothes off."

"Please," I plead with him, but only once. That's all I'm willing to give him.

He responds by pushing his jacket aside, his hand drawing his pistol. "You can do it by gun point or willingly. Your choice."

After a moment of hesitation, I pull the chemise over my head and let it drop to the floor. The bottle of laudanum lands with a *thud* on top of my shirt. Beak holsters his pistol again. The knife tucked in my garter falls to the floor along with my discarded skirt. I stand naked in front of him and cover my breasts by crossing my arms. He grabs me by my braid and turns me away from him. With his other hand, he pushes my arms down and caresses my chest, growling against my neck and biting my shoulder.

"Oh, I've been waiting for this," he says. "I've wanted you since I first saw you."

His cock presses against my ass. I look at the knife peeking from beneath my skirt on the floor, but I can't reach it. Beak pushes me down until my chest is on the bed. He uses one of his legs to wrench my thighs apart as he works the button of his pants. In a swift motion, he pulls himself out of the splayed fabric and finds his way inside me.

I guess the trick is to just be that hungry.

He groans as he thrusts his hips against me, shaking the bed and causing it to hit the wall. His rhythm is uneven and uncomfortable. He flips me onto my back.

"I want to see your face," he whispers with hot breath.

I defy him by turning my head away and looking at the wall. This isn't my first rodeo, and it probably won't be my last. I focus on the patterns of the wallpaper and look at a nail hole that cuts one of the patterns in half. I remain silent and retract myself into my mind until I'm no longer present at all.

I can't feel his hands, his cock, or his mouth. I can only smell the sweet smell of the apple I ate. I hang on to that scent as a source of comfort. If I stay calm, I will be able to eat another apple tomorrow. What a silly aspiration to hold on to.

Warm liquid slides down my thigh. Beak thrusts harder and grabs my face with a rough hand as he forces me to look at him. I look at him, but I can't see him as I dance within my own mind. He leans over and kisses me, but I don't kiss back. He slaps me, but I still refuse his mouth. His mustache rubs the skin above my lip raw as his lips spread against mine. He groans, and his thrusts hasten and then slow as he finishes.

"Don't pretend you're not a whore next time." He buttons his pants and spits. It lands near my feet.

The clanking sound of his belt buckle brings me back into my physical body. When he turns away, I reach for the knife, but I can't bring myself to stab him. I still don't know what the rules are here. Would I be protected or handed over to the sheriff? Would the madam release her hold on me?

I clutch the knife behind my back, and he turns toward me, tipping his hat before closing the door behind him. I drop to the floor, still naked. A few tears finally slip past my eyelashes.

There's a knock on the door, and a small figure appears in the doorway. I look up and see Belle as she runs over and drops to her knees beside me. She touches my face and wraps my skirt around me before gasping at the sight of the blood on the wooden floor beneath me.

"Oh, Hannah. What happened?"

"Fucking Beak."

"Who?" She cocks her head.

"I don't know his real name. I call him Beak because of his huge fucking nose."

She stops for a moment to think. "Does he have long, light-colored hair?"

"Yes, that's him."

"Sounds like that piece of shit, Wallace Amernathy. You and I aren't the only ones he's done this to."

My eyes widen. "He raped you too?"

"Not long after I started working here, yes," she says.

"Why is he still allowed to come here? I thought we paid for protection?"

"If you spend enough money here, you can do whatever—or *whoever*—you want."

She brushes the hair from my face and helps me up, handing me my shirt. I slip it on before I pull the skirt over my red-tinged thighs.

"I'll go get you some hot water," she says.

I follow her into the hall and wait for her in my room. She enters with a steaming bowl of water in her hands. I sit on the bed, groaning in pain as I hike up my skirt and spread my thighs. The blood is smeared over my skin like battle stripes. Belle drops to the ground between my knees, and I forget about the pain for a moment as she gently scrubs at my skin with a rag.

"That piece of shit." She grits her teeth around the words. "Raped me a month after I got here. He did it again a while back, and the familiarity of his cock didn't make it any easier." Belle shakes her head and unintentionally takes out her frustration as she grinds the cloth into my skin, reddening my flesh. With a frustrated sigh, she drops the rag into the bowl, the water splashing up and spilling onto the floor. "I'm sorry," she says, touching the raw skin of my thigh.

Seeing Belle falter with frustration is hard to watch. She's usually so composed. Sexual assault does this to a person. We lay the blame on our bodies instead of his. His cock is a weapon, wounding us, yet the prison walls rise around ourselves instead of him.

CHAPTER NINE

I shuffle down the stairs, sore between my legs. I can't bring myself to put on more than a chemise and a skirt, but my pride hurts worse than my crotch. The sleeves fall down my shoulders, and it's about as much skin as I'm willing to show at this point.

Weston stands outside by his horse, talking to the madam. Her head bobbles like a doll, and by the look of his hand gestures, he's telling her to calm down. Her bobbling intensifies. He reaches out his hand, touches her arm, and smiles, which seems to calm her down. He has that way with people.

She sees me and motions me outside.

"This gentleman wants to take you out today," she says as she rattles coins in her hand. Her bracelets jingle against each other.

He can't keep paying for me. I'm not something that can be bought.

Louise steps aside, and Weston tips his hat at her. He puts a boot in the stirrup and mounts Concetta.

I walk over and rub a hand down the horse's neck. "I don't think I can get on a horse today, Wes."

"Are you okay?" His eyes scan me, looking for the issue.

"No."

He hops down, puts his hands on my shoulders, and looks at me until it feels as if he's looking *through* me. I know he can see the pain on my face—the twist of my mouth and the furrow of my brow.

"What if I cushion the saddle with my coat?" He shrugs his arms out of his thick wool jacket and lays it over the saddle, standing before me in his white undershirt.

I shake my head. I want to go with him, but I don't think my body can withstand any more rough handling.

"I just want to take you away from here for a little while," he whispers, caressing the cut on my cheek.

I nod, and he helps me up. I sit down as softly as I can. He hops up behind me and puts his arms around my waist.

"I can't say that I've ridden like this since I was a wee one." He laughs and shows me how to hold the reins.

I look down at the powerful beast beneath me. "How do I get her to go?"

"Squeeze her sides."

I squeeze as hard as I can without sending pain searing up my thighs and pelvis, but Concetta doesn't move forward.

"I can't," I whine, and he taps her sides with his spurs.

She walks forward.

"Guess she might be a little dead to the leg by now," he says.

Every step Concetta takes jars my insides, but a little pain never killed anyone. He urges her into a trot.

"I'm going to fall!" I scream.

"No you aren't. I have you."

He pushes her into a canter, and I rock with her motion. His jacket cushions the area between my legs, and the warm heat of it soothes me. He puts his hat on my head, and I hold it with one hand.

"Now you're a cowgirl."

When we reach the house, Concetta slows to a walk and whinnies. Weston slides off the side of her, looking almost as clumsy as when I did it. He reaches his hand up, and I flinch as he helps me dismount. He supports my weight until I'm almost to the ground, putting me down gently. We walk to the porch, where he's placed two of the wooden house chairs. He motions for me to sit, and when I do, he sits next to me.

"We have to talk," we say in unison, but he motions for me to go first.

"You can't buy me, Wes." I look up at him, and his rich brown eyes intoxicate and distract me.

He plucks the hat from my head and puts it back on his. "I didn't buy you. If I did, I wouldn't have to bring you back." He gives me a coy smile.

"You know what I mean. You're spending too much money to 'rent' me." I sigh.

"If that's the only way I can spend time with you, so be it. It's just money." He puts his hand over mine. "Now, what I want to talk about is what happened to you." He reaches over and touches the cut on my cheek.

"You don't need to worry about that."

He grabs my chin and forces me to look at him. There's a whole lot of force around here. "Hannah, tell me."

I breathe deeply and nibble the inside of my cheek. "I was raped."

He rises to his feet and takes a few steps forward, staring at the desert landscape instead of looking at me. "When?" he asks as he puts his hand up to his mouth, caressing his beard. His posture is rigid.

"Yesterday," I tell him, my cheeks flushing.

"Who did it?"

"You might know him. I think his name is Wallace."

He turns to look at me with his mouth agape. "Wallace? The guy at the poker table when I met you?"

I nod and drop my gaze in shame, the filthy hands of that man still fresh in my memory.

"That son of a bitch!"

Weston walks toward Concetta, but I stand up and grab his arm.

"Don't!" I lock eyes with him, my lips trembling.

"I can't just let him get away with that!"

He shakes his arm out of my grasp and starts to unhitch his horse, but I put my hand over his and lean into him. I wrap my arm around his waist and pull him into me.

"I can't let you do anything, Wes. This isn't who you are."

"You don't even know me," he says without thinking. He looks down, and his hat obscures his eyes, so I lift his chin.

Something bubbles beneath his surface. He's strong, smart, and has superior skills when it comes to his pistol. I don't think he's just a rancher, but I'm also not just a saloon girl. I wish I could tell him who Hannah is. The person in front of him is a walking fabrication. I'm too afraid to show him who I really am because he'll think I'm crazy. Maybe I am.

"That may be so, but I want to know you." I smile at him, and he rests his chin against my head. I'm used to telling a man whatever I have to in order to calm him down.

"I do too," he whispers, almost too low to hear. His body relaxes against mine.

Wes takes a step backward, holds me at arm's length, and smirks. He tries to change the subject. "Do you want to see what I wanted you to do today?" He doesn't stay to hear my response. "Wait right here!" He calls back as he walks away.

He disappears behind the house, and I hear a bleating sound as he comes back around the corner. In one hand, he leads a brown goat by a leash made of twine. In the other, he holds a bucket.

"I am not—" I say as I wave my hand at him, dismissing his idea.

"Oh, you are!" He laughs as he ties the twine to the railing of the porch and puts the bucket down next to the goat. He takes a seat on the porch and crosses his legs. "Go on."

I walk over and squat down beside the goat with a shake of my head. Two swollen teats dangle from her underside. I rub a hand down her coarse chocolate coat. "I don't know what to do with it!" I yell with a squeal.

"Just give 'er a squeeze!"

I roll my eyes and touch one of the udders, but my hand recoils. *Oh, I don't like this.* "There's only one thing I like to milk," I whisper.

"What did you say, dear?"

"Nothing!"

I wrap my hand around an udder and squeeze, and the goat bleats in protest. After trying my hand in different positions, I manage to pull milk from the teat. It streams out, squirting into the bucket with a low *whoosh*.

"Oh, I got it!" I shout.

Weston applauds.

When I've finished, I bring him the half-full bucket of milk and collapse in his lap. "What are you trying to do? Make a wife out of me?" I drop my head back and sigh dramatically.

"What if I am?"

Belle's words fill my head. *No one wants to wed a whore.*

Weston wipes the sweat from my brow. "You're burning up." He uses the back of his hand to touch the skin of my forehead and chest.

"I can't say I get much sun, aside from here," I say as I lift my sun-kissed, porcelain arms.

"Sit down," Wes says, standing and gesturing toward the chair.

He unties the goat and walks her to the back of the house. He returns with another bucket and kneels beside me, pulling a flannel cloth from his pocket. With sure hands, he dips it in the bucket. I close my eyes as he dabs my chest with the cool water. After wetting the cloth again, he wipes it along my forehead and cheeks, stopping at my lips. His hand hovers there.

He leans closer, and his mouth seeks mine as I let him kiss me. He drops the rag and puts both hands behind my neck, sending water droplets down the back of my shirt. I shiver and pull away from him. I can't open my heart to a man in my own time, let alone here. My jaded feelings toward love came with me through that motel room door.

"I have to get back, Weston."

"So soon?" he asks. "Let me cook you up something first." His fingers graze my collarbone. "You're skin and bones."

Skin and bones? I've lost weight since I've been here, but I needed to lose a few pounds anyway. The longer I'm here, the closer I get to the body I wish I had in my time—the fragile body of a whore.

"I can't, Wes."

He frowns at me before standing and wiping the water off on his pants. The milk sloshes against the metal sides of the bucket as he lifts it and disappears into the house.

The sounds of rattling metal and tinkling glass reach my ears. Curiosity gets the better of me, and I follow Wes inside with a groan. A pungent aroma assaults my senses, and my hand flies up to my nose.

"What's that smell?" I ask, breathing through my mouth.

Wes pours a small amount of clear liquid into the bucket of milk and places the glass back onto the table. "I'm preserving the milk."

"With what? Rotten pickle juice?" I gag.

"No, don't be silly. It's formaldehyde." He grunts as he tightens the lid on the bottle.

"Did you just say formaldehyde?" I take a step back. "That shit causes *all* the cancer, Wes."

"No it doesn't." He chuckles as he puts the jar on the ground and pushes it toward the wall.

"It most certainly does. Where I'm from, you aren't even supposed to smell this stuff, let alone put it in your damn milk!" I make a mental note: do not drink the milk here.

"I'm sorry I don't have the fancy stuff you guys have in New York."

I roll my eyes at his snarky remark. "It has nothing to do with New York or Arizona. It has to do with over a century of research into the toxicity of formaldehyde. They use it to preserve dead bodies!"

"Century? I don't think it's been around that long. You're talking strange."

I swallow hard, realizing the mistake I made with my words. I almost gave up my biggest secret, and I'm not prepared to expose that part of who I am yet.

"Just forget it, Wes. I need to get back."

"I know. Come on." Wes wipes his hands on his shirt before wrapping his arm around me. The scent of formaldehyde carries back with us to the Bawdy.

CHAPTER TEN

"Hannah?" Belle says as I groan and turn away from her voice. "Hannah? Wake up!" She shakes my shoulder.

"What?" I turn toward her, speaking more harshly than I intended.

"Wallace is dead," she says with a grin.

I sit up, wipe my eyes, and look at her. Her smile spreads across her face, big and toothy. She's nearly wiggling with excitement.

"What do you mean he's dead?" I ask with raised eyebrows.

"Like dead dead. Gunned down right out front! He has a bullet through his head." She points to the front of her head, mimics his death, and laughs.

My heart sinks because I know who did it. Part of me is glad that prick is dead, but the other part is concerned that such darkness could be inside Wes. Maybe he didn't do it, though. Wallace seemed like the type of guy who made easy enemies.

Belle eyes my partially open dresser drawer. She spots the bottle of laudanum, and her eyes light up. "May I?"

I nod, and she opens it and uses the dropper on her tongue. Her pupils pinpoint. She sits down next to me before handing me the bottle. "Only use a little bit. One teaspoon is enough to kill you."

I drip the liquid onto my tongue and lean back against the headboard. Euphoria. Belle turns toward me and smiles before touching my cheek. She leans in to kiss me, her lips spreading as her tongue explores mine. I undo the ties on her chemise. The fabric opens, exposing her breasts. I kiss the soft porcelain skin of her chest and tease her with my tongue. I caress her breasts before finding her lips again. She moans against my mouth.

"We can't do this, Hannah." She groans and pushes me away.

"I know," I say with frustration as I kiss down her neck and nibble on her collarbone.

No matter how many men she's taken to bed, I find her to be as pure as snow. She's quiet and alluring—the whore I wish I could be.

Wes pushes his way into my mind, galloping in with heavy hoofbeats and a silent tip of his hat. Despite his entrance, feelings of inadequacy rise until they suffocate me. I'm incapable of loving him, Belle, or even myself.

"I'm sorry," I say, scooting away from her.

She smiles at me as she ties her chemise, pulling loose strands of hair from the knot. "Don't apologize. I can tell you have your mind on something or someone else, anyway." She drops her gaze for a moment. Is it from jealousy? The same green monster I feel when I see her hanging on the arm of a filthy client?

She's right, though. I lost sight of her face as Weston's

replaced it. The depth of his brown eyes overpowered the shallow blue of hers. My heart thumps in a confused rhythm.

She kisses me one last time before leaving me alone in my room.

I let out a deep sigh and lie back on my bed, feeling an aching in my gut and a throbbing between my legs. I reach my hand down my shorts and play with myself, rocking against my hand with the powerful imagery of Belle's arching body. Heat rises in my abdomen, but I can't come. With a frustrated groan, I stand up and pull on a skirt, tucking my chemise into it.

I walk out the door and almost run into Ivy. She eyes me with her usual distrust, but she enters her room and closes her door without saying a word to me. I walk down to the saloon and see the sheriff just outside the doors. He's hovering over Wallace's body, which still lies where he fell. Blood has pooled by his head, and his skin is mottled. I walk outside and cover my nose as the metallic scent crawls toward me.

"I see you've settled in well, miss," the sheriff says, tipping his hat.

"Yes, I guess so. What happened here?"

"Just a shooting, ma'am. Nothing you need to worry your pretty head about." He says this as if the women here are not to be bothered with such matters. It's insulting.

"Do you have any suspects?" *Because I do.*

"No, whoever shot him hightailed it out of here before anyone saw."

I sigh with relief and turn toward the sound of approaching hoofbeats. Weston rides up and grins down at me.

"Oh my, what happened here?" he says in a teasing tone. He smiles and reaches his hand down to me. "Do you care to go for a ride?"

"I don't really think that's a good idea, Weston." I look over at Wallace's body. The noon sun roasts his flesh in the heat. His dirty hair splays around him, caked with mud and blood.

"Oh, come on. This town seems very unsafe right now. I mean, there's a murderer on the loose!"

I roll my eyes, take his hand, and clamber up. I still have an aching in my gut from earlier, my orgasm trapped somewhere between my mind and my pussy. I wrap my arms around him, and Concetta takes a few steps before breaking into a canter.

As we ride out of town, my arm grazes the pistol on his hip, and I shiver. *Did this gun kill Beak?* I stare ahead as we travel the winding road up to his farm. Vultures pick apart the corpse of a fallen coyote not far from his home.

When we arrive at the farm, I dismount and tug at his arm. "Are we going to talk about this?"

"Talk about what?" He hops down and begins removing Concetta's tack without meeting my eyes.

"How you fucking killed Wallace?" I'm unwilling to play any games. We're talking about murder, after all.

He stops mid-step and stares at me, putting his hand to his chest. "Me?"

"Yes, you. I didn't tell anyone else about what he did." Besides Belle. I did tell Belle, but she didn't have the means or the opportunity to do it. I know it was Wes, and I'm not sure how it makes me feel.

"Wallace was a very hated man, Hannah. It could have been anyone," he says, dismissing my theory.

"What is this if we can't be honest with each other, Wes?" I fold my arms across my chest. For a moment, my thoughts drift to the lies I've told so far. My entire existence here is a lie.

He reaches for my chin, but I pull away from him. "Fine. I shot Wallace." He speaks so quietly, I almost can't hear him.

"What?" I hold my hand up to my ear, mocking him.

"I shot Wallace, but I did it for you."

"I didn't ask you to! In fact, I think I explicitly told you *not* to!"

"He violated you!" He raises his voice at me.

I lower my head as a tear drifts down my cheek. Being a knight in tarnished armor does nothing for me, and I don't appreciate the gesture. Violence is why I'm the way I am to begin with. If he only knew how many Wallaces there have been . . . there wouldn't be enough bullets. My honor doesn't need defending, anyway. It departed long before Wallace came along.

He pulls me into him despite my protests, his breath heavy on the back of my neck. I sense a darkness in him that I never noticed before. Whatever was boiling beneath the surface has spilled over. He lifts my chin and caresses my cheek, and my eyes close. Maybe it's not who he is, but who he fights to keep from becoming.

"So, I was thinking . . . why don't we go drive some of the cattle?" He tries to change the subject and redirect me.

"Isn't there something I could do here instead?" I groan.

"And leave you alone again? Not a chance. Are you trying to get more blood on my hands?" He smirks and walks into his house with me. He rustles through the drawers near his bed and pulls out a crimson skirt. The shade of red is almost the color of Wallace's blood.

I shiver.

"One of Mary's split skirts," he says, handing it to me. "You can't drive cattle in a normal skirt."

I feel guilty holding the fabric in my hands. Mary is probably turning in her grave at the thought of a whore wearing her clothes.

"Let me know if they don't fit," Weston says as he steps outside.

I slip off my skirt, fold it neatly on the bed, and pull the red fabric of the split skirt up my legs. *Oh, it has pant legs! I haven't gotten to wear pants since I came here!* When I'm standing, it looks just like my skirt, but when I spread my legs, the layers visibly separate into pants. I walk out and see Wes standing by the door.

"These are pants!" I say with a grin, unable to contain my excitement.

"No ma'am. They are not," he corrects me.

"They are." I refuse to be swayed on the matter.

He laughs and wraps his arm around me as we walk toward the horse corral. He twirls his mustache for a moment in thought as he decides. "I think I'll have you ride Concetta. I'll take Hickock."

The large red gelding paws the ground as Weston removes the saddle from Concetta and places it on his back instead. Wes hands the reins to me while he goes to get Mary's old saddle out of the barn. I run my hand along the white blaze on the horse's face. His chestnut coat mesmerizes me. I lead him toward Weston, who's saddling Concetta with Mary's smaller saddle. He holds her steady as I put my foot in the stirrup and mount her.

He struggles a bit to get on top of Hickock; he looks twice the size of Concetta. He perches himself in the saddle and looks down at me. "You ready?"

"Ready as I'll ever be, I guess." I sigh.

Weston passes me a cowboy hat. I run my fingertips along the soft, well-worn leather before putting it on my head and slipping my braided hair over my shoulder. Wes and Hickock start in the direction of the sun, and I shield my eyes as Concetta follows the massive red horse.

"Where are we going?" I ask.

"A couple miles south of here."

We don't talk much more as we pick up speed on the horses. I hold my hat down on my head to keep it from blowing off. After a long ride, we spot the brown and black cattle. Half have twisted horns rising from each side of their heads. They keep their noses to the ground, grazing along the dusty earth.

"They're kind of lanky, aren't they?" I ask, cocking my head at the thin cows. They're nothing like I'm used to seeing.

"They're Criollos. They're built for the desert environment here. They'll eat the tumbleweeds and prickly pears, unlike most cattle."

"What are we doing with them?"

"Driving them back to the farm, into the pen behind the barn. I'm selling some off to the butcher."

I feel a pang of sadness for them, even though I know it's the circle of life. One of the cows bellows as I ride Concetta toward it, kicking up sand as it walks away. "So what do we do?"

"We flank them on each side. They'll move together as a herd." He tries to explain, but I just stare at him blankly. He rolls his eyes. "We'll just get behind them. Let's go."

I lift the cowboy hat to wipe the sweat from my forehead before following after him. We face our horses toward the herd, and Weston starts driving them forward.

"*Hyup,* let's go. *Hyup!*" His voice is deep, and the cattle respond by walking forward.

I ride Concetta on the right side of the herd while Weston keeps them contained on the left. He urges Hickock into a trot, and I follow suit, bouncing on Concetta's poor back. I grab the saddle horn with one hand and try to sit deeper into the saddle. The hot leather rubs against my tailbone, but it's nothing I can't handle. This is still better than being at the Bawdy.

The cattle speed up, bellowing in defiance. Some of the younger animals start to fall behind the herd. A calf trails in the back and nearly gets left behind.

"Yell at it. Get 'em moving," Weston yells to me.

"Come on, get going!" I say. The little calf continues at the same pace.

"Deep and guttural noises, Hannah. They don't respond to suggestions."

I clear my throat and try to mimic the noises slipping past Weston's soft lips, but I feel embarrassed at the sounds erupting from my mouth. *"Hyup, hyup!"*

The little calf speeds up and rejoins his herd.

"Atta girl!" Weston smiles at me.

The pen waits ahead of us with the gate wide open.

"How do we make them go in?" I yell.

"We get closer together. They'll head right for the opening."

As the distance closes, Weston pulls Hickock up a bit. The horse snorts in defiance but falls in line next to me, and we drive the cattle toward the pen. They file into it and make a beeline for the hay. As they munch away, Weston hops down and closes the gate, tying it to a post with a length of twine from his pocket.

He turns to me with a smile across his face and slaps his thigh. "That was a beautiful drive! I wish they all went like that." He walks over to Concetta and pats her side. Her coat is soaked with sweat. "Did you take care of my girl?"

I glance down at Concetta, unsure which one of us is "his girl." I let the moment pass without an answer. I dismount and almost fall once I reach the ground. I can't feel my legs.

Wes catches me and makes sure I'm steady before he

releases his hold. "Whoa, there. Maybe we went a little too hard."

"I think that's the most exercise I've done in my entire life." I put my hands on the seat of the split skirt. The fabric is so sweat soaked, it feels and looks like I peed my pants. The skin of my arms and chest flush red from the sun's dangerous kiss. I breathe deeply and put my hands on my hips.

After helping remove the horses' tack, I collapse onto a chair on the porch with my legs splayed in the most unfeminine way.

"You know, that's not very ladylike," he says, smiling sideways at me.

"Well, I hate to break it to you, Wes, but I'm not very ladylike."

He laughs and covers my hand with his. His skin is warm and tanned. "You sure aren't like anyone else I've ever met."

I smile and look toward the sun. "It's getting late. I really need to get back."

"I need to tell you something." Wes turns toward me and rubs the skin of my hand with his fingers. I can see the concern in his eyes. "I don't have money to pay you right now."

"What? I . . . Weston . . ." I stumble over my words.

"I'm sorry. I'm selling off a few of the cattle for some extra money."

I shake my head, my jaw slack and eyes wide. "Why would you take me away from the Bawdy if you knew you couldn't pay?"

"I just wanted to see you," he rubs a hand along the fabric of his pants, trying to avoid my gaze.

I pull my hand away and place it in my lap. I turn away from him and stare at the mountains as I fight back tears.

"It's not about the money, Wes. I would spend my time with you for free. It's that I have a debt to pay."

"I know," he says.

"No, you don't know. You don't have any idea what I'll have to do for the rest of that money." My shoulders fall forward.

Of course he knows what I'll have to do for that money. Yet he still put me in this situation. Why would he do this?

"Just stay here. With me." There's hope in his voice.

"I can't, Wes." I sigh, realizing what he'd hoped to achieve. My lip trembles. I can't leave the Bawdy. It's the only chance I have of getting home.

CHAPTER ELEVEN

I walk into the lounge and find the madam sitting with one leg perched on the table. She uses a silk folding fan to cool her face, sending wisps of her hair blowing back. It is extraordinarily hot today. Most of the girls— including myself—wear only a chemise and undergarments. It's not the most attractive look.

"Madam?"

She doesn't look up at me as she continues fanning herself. "What, Hannah?"

I purse my lips and take a deep breath. "I'm going to be short this week."

She closes the fan and places it on her lap before turning toward me and staring. The corners of her mouth threaten to lift upward. "Your little rancher can't afford to keep you around?" She chuckles, pulling her lips together again in a tight line.

"He'll have the money soon." I try to believe my own words.

"So, what're we going to do about this now?"

I suck in my cheeks and drop my gaze to the floor. "I'm willing to take on a client. But only one!"

She smiles with painted lips, as if she enjoys it when I have to ask for permission to take a man to bed. I have no choice but to give her the power she craves.

"That arrangement could work. In fact, I have a very special man in mind." She smiles.

I shake my head at her. "I choose my clients."

"He'll pay top dollar." She rises to her feet, her chin lifting slightly.

I look at her for a moment while I argue with myself about taking on a client chosen by the madam. If I take on a well-paying client—even just one—I might not have to take on another, even if Weston can't pay next time. But if I take on someone the madam chooses, I defy the one rule I've had since I ended up here.

I sigh. It wouldn't be the first time I've let money choose my client for me, so I nod to her.

"Go get dressed up," she says, waving me off. "You can't look like that for this client."

Today? In this heat? Instead of arguing, I walk back to my room and put on my dark green dress. I slip on my stockings, followed by my garters. There's soft white flesh just above the lace. To appease the warm sweat on the back of my neck, I wrap my hair into a bun.

There's a knock on my door, and the madam comes in with the client hooked on her arm. *Was he already here? Why?* He looks as if he's in his thirties, with fiercely attractive features and gently tousled blonde hair. He wears a vest and jacket over a white undershirt. A splash of blue around his neck comes from a silk neckerchief.

"Holden, this is Hannah," Madame Louise says.

His bright-blue eyes scan my body up and down, seeking out

my flaws. His expression is blank, but at least he doesn't wear an expression of disapproval. Several seconds pass as he tries to determine if I'm really worth the money I'm asking for. He continues staring, determining if the cracks in my exterior are possible to overlook—or enjoy. I despise this part of escorting.

Madam Louise looks at me. "This is Holden. He owns the Bawdy."

I had no idea it was owned by someone else. I've been assuming it belonged to Louise. She coos as she speaks of him, and for a moment, I wonder if he may be her son.

"She's the one who's unsoiled?" He looks down at the madam, and she shoots me a glare as she nods.

"Yes, she is." She fixes the man's neckerchief and smiles. "I'll leave you two to get to know each other."

Louise leaves the room, and I'm left alone with Holden. He doesn't seem bothered by all the clothing he wears, even in this heat. The layers of fabric I wear are almost unbearable. I wipe sweat off my forehead.

He sits on the bed and motions for me to sit beside him. "Louise has told me all about you."

"Oh?" I say with faked flirtation.

"Yes. You're the woman who comes to a bordello and refuses to lie on her back. It's fascinating to me." He touches my cheek for a moment. "Do you know how many women are in this town? Not many. Do you know how many are unsoiled? Just you. I hear you're willful, spirited, and resourceful. Unbreakable, even." He leans closer until his lips are beside my ear. "I want to shatter you," he whispers.

I look at him with wide eyes. I'd agree that I'm resourceful and unbreakable, but I'm not following him regarding his desire to "shatter" me. He stands and lifts me up by my throat without being too rough. He trails his hand down my neck and the front of my dress, and he caresses my breasts.

"Oh, you are stunning," he whispers as he grabs my face with his other hand. His fingers interlace with my hair. He cranes my neck, draws back his hand, and slaps me across the face before rubbing my cheek softly.

I whimper against his touch, my body confused by the conflicting sensations. Holden lays me on my back and fumbles with the button of his pants. His slacks fall to his feet. He steps out of them and kicks them aside and, with a quick motion, he presses himself inside me. I gasp. He's girthy, and I'm surprised I couldn't see such a monster through his pants. Maybe it was the pinstripes.

Holding on to the bunched fabric of my dress, he slams into me. He brandishes a small razor and looks up at me with cold, starving eyes. I grab his wrist, trying to push away the blade. He shakes my hand from his arm, despite my nails digging into him. His weight holds me down and stops my thrashing panic beneath him. He slides the razor along the skin of my chest while keeping me pinned. I bite back a scream. My skin separates and the channel fills with deep-red liquid. He laps at the wound with his tongue, and I try to push him away again, but he holds me down by my wrists. This isn't the first time a knife has seared my flesh to heighten a man's pleasure. Faded scars mar the skin above my breasts.

"I didn't agree to this." My voice is panicked.

He laughs. "It doesn't matter what you agreed to. I paid to do whatever I desire. If I wanted to gut you like a fucking deer, I could. If I wanted to cut across that sweet, soft flesh of your neck, I could." He reaches up and touches the throbbing artery in my neck. With a groan, he closes his eyes.

He takes the razor and slices beneath the first cut, and I wince as my flesh spills its blood. He draws his tongue back to my wound. I wiggle out of his grasp and try to stand, but he punches me in the face so hard that my vision blurs and the room darkens. I close my eyes to stave off the pain as he moves my limp body into the position he wants.

I open my eyes again with a nauseating dizziness and pain in my head. I'm on my stomach now, and he's pulling me back by my hair.

"Don't you pass out on me, sweetheart. Not yet." He reaches up to his neck and unties his scarf, grasping one side in each hand. In a swift movement, he wraps it around my throat.

I reach up, trying without success to slip one hand between the silk and my throat. He twists the scarf until my breath is cut off. My chest heaves as I try to get away from him. As I claw at the scarf, his thrusts grow hard and fast. He continues pulling me toward him until I start to lose consciousness. My head falls forward, and when my eyes start to close, I will myself awake. I can't die like this, in this time, with this person.

He finishes as I feel the strain of my lungs pleading for their final breath. He releases the scarf, and I suck in air, coughing. He stands and steps into his discarded pants, leaving me on the bed, panting and clutching my neck.

"Are you broken yet, sweetheart?" His voice is low and sultry as his fingers curl and graze my cheek.

He has evil inside of him that he hides from everyone but himself and the madam—deep and dark fantasies that are too taboo for this age. If he traveled to my time, he'd find women who live to be choked and are just as into blood play as he is. Alas, he's stuck in a time where even oral sex is forbidden.

I feel a little bad for him because I can't imagine having to hide such an intense part of myself. Sympathy toward my clients is something I've never been able to stop, even when they do awful things to my body. Their reasons for hurting me are often buried and deeply personal.

Before leaving the room, he pats my head the way a

parent does to console a small child. The door slams behind him.

I sob into my pillows as I reach over and fumble for the bottle of laudanum in the dresser drawer. I drip several drops onto my tongue. My body and mind relax in a way that only opiates can accomplish.

It relieves the ache on my face, around my neck, and between my legs. It comforts the agony within my head, and smothers the prying thoughts of suicide that come from the abuse we women face every day here. Do I want to die? No. But I also don't want to live like this anymore. I don't know what's worse: Wes finding my body bruised and bleeding like this or knowing that someone like Belle has felt similar harsh hands and rough thrusts. A nine-to-five job doesn't seem so arduous after all.

CHAPTER TWELVE

In the hallway, Belle gasps at the sight of the black-and-blue bruise creeping across the left side of my face. It runs from my cheek to my eye. She covers her mouth at the sight of the deep cuts across my chest.

"What happened, Hannah?"

"I met Holden." My lip curls at the mention of his name.

"He did that to you? He seems so kind . . ."

"Well, he's not." I want to call him sick, but I can't quite bring myself to say it. Having kinks doesn't make you sick. We can't help what turns us on. What makes him sick is how he forces his fetishes on someone who isn't willing. His kinks weren't even the strangest I'd been a part of. For the right money, I would have done it consensually.

Belle reaches her hand out and touches my cheek, and I breathe in her scent. She smells like lavender with a subtle hint of tobacco.

"Are you okay?" she asks. Her eyes are transfixed. A tear slips past her eyelids and paints a streak down her cheek.

I want to reach over and wrap her up in my arms. Her

emotional pain overshadows my physical pain; it's more deep-seated. She lets herself cry as she sobs into my chest, and her tears soak through my shirt. I can feel her warmth and vulnerability.

"I'll be ok," I say. "We have to be unbreakable."

She fakes a smile. There's a familiar sadness behind her eyes. I wish I could have met Belle in my own time. She has such a soft demeanor, as if she's an old soul. She's been beaten down so many times, yet she still managed to become a softer person instead of hardening from such abuse. I chose this lifestyle of my own free will, so I feel a sense of culpability when things go awry. Belle was forced into prostitution against her will. Every client leaves her more and more shattered.

That's what Holden meant.

"Well, I feel like I'm breaking, Hannah." She wipes away the tears before they drip onto the skin of my chest. Her body is heavy against my embrace, as if I'm holding her up.

What can I say to comfort her? I'm just as broken.

"I know, Belle. But you aren't. I'll do whatever I can to keep you together."

I'm not sure I would go through the door back to my time if it opened in front of me right now. Hearing that Belle has reached this familiar point ignites my desire to protect her— to be a light for her in this darkness.

She opens her mouth as if she's going to speak, but she decides against it.

There's a knock on the door, and Ivy's gruff voice comes from the other side. "Did you forget about the miners coming through?"

Belle blinks hard. "I didn't forget. I'm coming." With a sigh, she gets up to leave, rubbing her eyes and smoothing her skirt.

When I no longer hear her footsteps, I stand and put my fist into the wall by the door. The wood bends but doesn't break. I grab a framed picture off the wall and toss it onto the ground. I can't stay in this place. But I also can't leave. Not yet.

I leave my room and glance at the lounge area. Belle sits on the lap of a weathered miner. With a painful concoction of jealousy and anger rising inside me, I head to the bar to soothe the beast.

I ask the bartender for a drink, and he stares at my face as he pours the whiskey. He shakes his head. I'm not sure if he's looking at me with concern or distaste. I lift the glass to my lips, toss my head back, and let the warm liquid fill my throat.

I hear Weston's voice asking around for me. I turn back to the bar and avoid his gaze, touching the bruise on my cheek. His voice fades, and I groan as I follow the trailing sound outside. He paces the wooden steps of the saloon's porch. The smile on his face disappears when he gets a closer look at me.

"Weston?"

He wraps me into a hug until I can't tell whose breaths are whose. His body tenses, and he breaks our embrace. He stands with his hand on his pistol, eyebrows drawn together and lips tight.

"Who did this? Is he in there?" His fingers wrap around the pistol's grip.

"No, Weston."

"Is he in there, Hannah?" He repeats himself with a harshness I haven't heard before, and I put my hand over his in hopes of keeping him from drawing his weapon.

"No, he's not!"

He closes his eyes for a moment and takes a deep breath. "What happened to you?"

I grab him by the arm of his jacket and pull him away from the door. "Don't ask me that here." I tap my ear and point toward the door. Ivy would love the opportunity to narc on me.

"Then come on. We have to go." Wes gestures toward his horse. He walks to Concetta and mounts her. With his eyes locked on the saloon doors, he reaches his hand down to help me up.

I hesitate, looking back at the Bawdy.

"Now," he commands. His tone sends a shiver up my spine and leaves no room for argument.

I groan before taking his hand and climbing on Concetta.

"Hang on," he tells me through a clenched jaw.

I wrap my arms around his waist, and he kicks Concetta into a canter.

"Don't kick her like that!"

"Not now." His voice is gruff, and he almost sounds like a stranger.

We don't speak the rest of the way. His posture is rigid and tense, as if he were fighting a detonation of anger. When we get to his farm, he dismounts and walks into the house without looking back at me, his anger apparent in every step.

"Oh, don't worry. I'll get myself down, thanks." I slide down Concetta's rump, walk her toward the pen, and let her through the gate before chasing after Wes. "What the fuck, Weston?"

"You aren't going back there," he says as soon as I walk through the door. He presses his body against mine, pinning me against the wall.

"The fuck I'm not."

He extends his arm, and his hand presses flat against the wood behind me. "I can't stand seeing you hurt."

His posture is threatening, but his words are kind, making it difficult to read this situation. He almost seems like two different people wrapped into one. On one hand, he's a gentle, compassionate, and endearing human being. On the other, he's a man willing to murder. Does it matter if he committed the murder because of his fondness for me? Does it make a difference if he shot a despicable rapist? I know in the eyes of modern law it doesn't, but we aren't in a modern world anymore.

He touches the bruise on my face. The nerves of my skin fire indiscriminately, and I flinch. His fingers trace down my neck and touch the purple bruises. In a quick motion, he tugs down my chemise and exposes the cuts. He sucks in a quick breath.

"What the fuck happened to you?"

"Do you really want to know?" I look at him, hoping he'll say no.

"No, but I need to know." His hand trembles against the wall beside my head.

I duck under his arm and sit on the lumpy mattress of his bed. "Well, when I didn't have the money to pay board, I agreed to take on a gentleman, just one more time."

"Who was it?" His lip trembles and his gaze drops, blame washing over him like a tidal wave.

"Holden. I don't even know his last name." I look down at the floorboards below my feet.

"Holden, as in the owner of the Bawdy?"

I nod and wring the fabric of my skirt in my hands.

"He's so . . ."

"Kind? If I hear that one more time, I'm going to flip my shit. A person can act nice and not be a good person."

Weston groans.

"Do you consider yourself a good person, Wes?"

He plays with his hat in his hands, and his gaze drops. He sits beside me and kicks out his feet.

I reach over and grab his chin, forcing him to look at me. "Tell me."

He shakes his head. "I can't, Hannah."

He lies back on the bed and covers his face with his hat. I lie next to him and rest my head on his chest. It rises and falls rhythmically as he wraps his arm around me and squeezes.

"I really don't want to let you go back there," he whispers.

"I have to go back there. There's no other place for a whore." There's no other place for Belle, and I can't leave her to fend off the wolves by herself.

He lifts the hat and places it next to him on the bed before sitting up and pulling me toward him. "You aren't a whore. You haven't even tried to sleep with me. If I remember correctly, you told me no."

"That doesn't mean I haven't thought about it." My cheeks flush with heat, and we both laugh. I would be described as a whore in this time as well as my own. Despite my attempt at modesty here, I have lain with too many men to be considered anything else.

"What if I refuse to bring you back?"

"That, sir, is called kidnapping."

He leans down and kisses my neck. His lips graze the frayed nerves hiding beneath the purple coloration. I crane my neck and let him explore as his hand reaches for the string of my chemise. He starts to loosen it, tempting my breasts to erupt from the fabric. I grab his hand, pull it away from me, and drop my head onto his chest.

Why do I keep stopping him? I have few qualms about giving myself up to any man, yet here I am, turning Weston away.

"I'm sorry, Wes."

He gives me a final kiss on my lips. "Is there anything I can do to convince you to stay?"

He leans on his elbow, his length painfully apparent along the front of his pants. My eyes are glued to the curves of what is beneath the fabric. As much as I want to say yes, I have to say no. Belle is breaking, and I can't stay here while she comes apart at the Bawdy.

Chapter Thirteen

I grab the beers off the counter, spilling some in my haste. The bartender gestures toward the men standing by the piano. I walk over to them with an accentuated sway of my hips. The older man grabs the beers and laughs, working to chug both as quickly as he can.

"Oh, do you want some?" he asks, flashing his rotten teeth at me. He wraps his hand around my waist and pulls me into him, spilling the beer down the front of my dress. The aroma of yeast and hops is unbearably strong. When mixed with the scent of his body odor, it's too much for one nose to handle.

I fight back a gag. "For fuck's sake!" I yell.

I shake out of his grasp and turn back toward the bar. I walk right into Ivy's full chest. She squints her eyes at me.

"That's quite the mouth on you," she says. The condescension in her voice is as big as her breasts. "If Madam heard you talk to clients like that . . ." She completes the sentence with her tongue by clicking it against the roof of her mouth as she shakes her head.

Sarah pops out from around the piano. "What did she say?"

Here we go.

"She just yelled at a client over a spilled drink!" Ivy says with fake shock on her face.

Sarah shakes her head. "That's no way to talk to a paying customer," she says with a defiant pop of her hip. "We should probably let the madam know."

Ivy turns to me with a grotesque smile. "There's a small group of drifters coming in later tonight, and I'm sure they'd love to get their disgusting hands on someone like *you*."

I shiver at the thought. The drifters who come through town are always filthy. Dirt covers them from head to toe. Their clothes would probably stand up on their own . . . if they ever took them off. I could smell them from across the bar. I'm not one to talk shit about someone's hygiene, but the thought of *that* inside me is too much to fathom. Only the most underperforming girls will take them on when they come through. I can't imagine there's enough soap or water in this whole fucking town to wash away the smell of dirty dick. There's no way in hell I would *ever* take on a drifter, but it wouldn't stop Louise from trying.

I can't tell Sarah what I want to say, and I definitely can't grace Ivy with the uncouth words I would like to say to *her*, so I keep my mouth shut. I take whatever insult and degradation they have to throw at me in stride, lifting my chin higher.

The doors burst open and Wes walks into the saloon. He has a cool smile on his face, which makes me raise a brow at him.

"Excuse me, ladies," he says as he slips between them.

Their eyes fill with jealousy or anger—maybe a bit of both. Wes looks back at them, motioning with his head for them to leave. Ivy scoffs, and they whisper to each other as they walk away.

"What do you want, Wes?" My eyes shoot daggers at him. I'm glad to see him, but not so enthused about his entrance. I don't need more waves crashing down on me than I already have.

"I have something very special to show you," he says. He's smiling so wide that his cheeks dimple. "Let's go."

I roll my eyes and follow him out of the saloon. He helps me up on Concetta. I knock into the bedroll behind me and hear metal clanking together. "What are we doing?"

"You'll see."

"Do I want to see?"

"You do." Wes turns toward me and smirks.

Concetta takes off at a canter, the rocking motion guiding my hips. There's no point in fighting, and besides, wherever we're going is better than the Bawdy and whatever tsunami Ivy went off to conjure.

We ride in a direction I've never traveled. There are no roads or buildings in sight. The endless landscape continues on around us. The sun is falling in front of us, giving the sky an orange hue.

"It's going to get dark soon, Wes."

"It's fine. We got a couple more hours, I reckon."

"What the hell are we going to do for a couple of hours?" I whine.

Wes takes us over the ridge, and I see a lump of gray leaning against a wooden post.

"What is that?" I ask.

Before he can answer, realization washes over me. I recognize the fancy suit and the pale blue scarf. "Wes . . ." My mouth is agape. The smell of blood infiltrates my nose. As we get closer, I see Holden's head slumped forward, motionless.

"Did you kill him?" I cover my mouth with my hand, more in shock than fear.

Holden's face is a mess.

How the hell did he get the town's richest man tied up in the goddamn desert?

"I didn't kill him." Wes hops off Concetta and helps me down. He walks over to Holden, scaring off a circling vulture. Wes lifts him up by the hair and slaps his face. "Wake up!"

Holden stirs awake and begins to panic, straining against the ropes. He lets out a scream, and Wes punches him in the jaw. Holden stops screaming as his mouth fills with blood.

"Willebrand, you're fucking dead," he says as he spits blood onto his jacket.

"Wes, this isn't what I want," I say, my voice shaking.

"Well, Hannah, it's what I want. Look at your face! It's only fair." He turns back to Holden. "You like beating up on women, Mr. Bawdy?" He loosens the bedroll on the back of Concetta, revealing an axe and a knife. Wes picks up the knife and walks over to Holden. He stands behind him, lifting Holden's head and holding the blade to his face. "You like to cut them? Does it get you hard?" He doesn't wait for an answer. He drags the blade across Holden's face.

Holden screams as the blood pours from the deep wound. I swallow my own scream. This isn't what I want.

The men who hurt me—who steal away pieces of who I am—never face repercussions for their transgressions. I've often wondered if there was such a thing as having to atone for such sins. Wes is the judge, jury, and executioner here. He's the guardian I never asked for. I can't accept him murdering anyone in my honor. It's almost as bad as what they did to me. Maybe worse. This isn't vengeance. Wes shouldn't force retribution for a pain he never felt.

Another scream erupts from Holden as Wes cuts him again.

"Wes, stop!" I yell, finally letting the words leap from my tongue.

Wes stops and looks at me with drawn eyebrows. He stands upright and wipes the knife on his pants before walking over to me.

"After all he did to you? How?" he asks.

"Because this isn't going to fix what he did. *This* isn't going to heal any of my wounds."

"I'm not asking you to participate, but I'm not letting him do this to another woman. If you've seen what I've seen, you'd know why I can't."

"I haven't just seen it, Wes. I've lived it!" I draw a frustrated breath.

Wes pulls me into him. "I will kill anyone who hurts you or even thinks about touching you. Mark my words."

I relax into him, finding reassurance in this possessiveness. I've never had anyone to protect me.

Wes releases me and holds me out in front of him. "I won't play with him anymore, but I can't let him live. You have to understand that."

I know he can't. If we let him go, Holden would make sure one or both of us are hanged.

Wes kisses me before going back to Holden and ripping the crimson-stained scarf from his neck. "Those marks on your neck were from this, weren't they?" he asks me.

I don't respond. I can't. Instead, I turn around and look away.

Holden pleads for his life, his attempts growing louder until they become muffled. The straining sounds of suffocation and legs kicking the sand fill the air. The struggle lasts for much longer than I thought it would. Longer than my own did at the hands of Holden and that damn scarf.

In a dark, romantic kind of way, it was almost poetic.

CHAPTER FOURTEEN

I wake up in bed with Weston, and he stirs awake.

"We must have fallen asleep," he says as he yawns. His sweet smile contrasts with the sadistic grin I saw in the desert. His arm wraps around me, and I stare at his hands.

I can't help but imagine them tightening the scarf and extinguishing Holden's life. I nod away the creeping thoughts and look out the window, trying to gauge the time of day. The sun has started to lift above the horizon. The sky bursts with beautiful pink and orange hues.

"I have to go to the bathroom. Where is it?"

Weston stands, pulls a chamber pot from under the bed, and pushes it across the floor toward me. My eyes widen at his suggestion.

"You go to the bathroom in *here?*"

"What else would you do?" He cocks his head at me.

I sigh. Oh, what I would give to pee in a nice porcelain toilet with running water. It doesn't even have to be nice. Just something besides a wooden box or a pot on the floor.

"I can't do that. I would rather use the outhouse."

"You can go outside, I reckon," he says with a shrug of his shoulders.

I nod and get dressed with urgent, tapping footsteps before walking outside to do my business near the barn. While my skirt is hiked, I look at the surroundings.

Tan sand stretches as far as I can see. The wind rustles it up and whips it against my skin. Reddish rock formations dot the horizon, and everything in the forefront lies flat, aside from the sparse desert grass and cacti. There's an eerie silence—a staleness. Above me, vultures soar through the clear blue sky on their vast black wings. The sky reminds me of Belle's eyes, and I find myself smiling at the thought of her.

I walk back into the house with a relieved sigh and find Weston standing in the kitchen. "What did we do?" I ask as I sit down on the bed.

"Nothing he didn't deserve." He places a comforting kiss on my forehead. Such tenderness for someone capable of multiple murders.

"That may be so, but I still think it was wrong."

"No one has to suffer any consequences for taking a woman against her will. The sheriff is easy enough to pay to look away, but I won't turn a blind eye to it. Hate me for it if you want, but I'd do it again without hesitation."

The cause is noble, but it still doesn't make it right. He's not wrong about the sheriff, though. To no avail, I've tried to turn men in to the police. How can a person take the most intimate piece of you and then live their life freely while you're trapped by your memories? It's more than criminal.

"I really have to get back, Wes. I can't imagine a world where I don't get some kind of repercussion from this little sleepover. Kind of hard to explain that I'm not sleeping with you when I'm literally sleeping with you."

"Do you want coffee first?" He gestures toward the fireplace.

"Quit stalling."

"Can't blame a guy for trying." He shrugs and heads outside to tack up Concetta. When he comes back, he straps his gun belt around his waist.

"Why do you need that?" I gesture toward his gun.

"I don't go anywhere without it," he says as he adjusts the buckle.

We walk outside, and he helps me onto Concetta before mounting her. We travel back to town at a leisurely pace. I can feel his smile, despite only seeing the back of his head.

Up ahead, a wagon with a broken axle waits on the side of the road. Weston tenses at the sound of a whistle. Before I have time to register what's happening, two bandits on horseback have converged to block the path.

"Oh, look what we have here. Hello, again." Roy licks his lips and growls as he leans over and puts his arm across the horn of his saddle. His hat still has a hole in it. They draw their pistols and aim them at Wes, but he doesn't move.

"How about I take her into the back of the wagon, Roy, and you get the money off him." He gestures with the barrel of his pistol.

"But, Horace, why can't I take her, and you rob him?" he whines.

"Shut up, Roy."

Weston turns his head slightly toward me, his lips drawn tight. "Tuck in behind me," he whispers.

"Why?" I try to argue back.

Weston draws his pistol and fires a single shot through Horace's chest. As Weston's round leaves the chamber, Roy shoots back. Wes cocks his pistol and fires only once more, hitting Roy in the head. His horse takes off toward town as he falls off it. Horace is busy trying to plug the hole in his chest with his hand, but the blood saturates his shirt. His body succumbs to his injury, and he slumps forward.

When the dust settles, I see Wes trying to hide a dark stain on his right thigh.

"Are you shot?" I ask.

"Yup." He sounds so casual about it, like it's only a mild inconvenience. "Are you okay?"

I give myself a quick once over and nod. He clucks Concetta into a gallop, and we race back toward his house. When we pull up to his porch, Weston kicks his good leg over and shimmies to the ground. The stain on his pants has doubled in size. I slide down from Concetta and hook my arm around his to support him as we walk inside.

He unbuttons his pants and lets them fall to the floor once we're past the doorway. His leg is covered in fresh blood, and a gaping wound runs across the front of his thigh.

"I'm fine. It's just a flesh wound. It just grazed me." He sits down on the bed and covers his crotch with a pillow. "This isn't how I wanted you to see my dick."

"Oh, shush. Do you have any liquor?"

He points to the bottle sitting on top of his meat box. I grab the liquor, pop out the cork, and take a whiff.

"Oh my god! Did you make this yourself?"

"Yes."

With a shake of my head, I pour it over the gash in his leg. He bites his lip in pain and leans backward. His breaths are quick and shallow as I soak up the pink tinged liquid with his discarded pants.

"The bullet hurt less than this."

I roll my eyes and wrap his thigh with an old undershirt that was lying on the floor. I catch a glimpse of his cock from under the pillow, mere inches from my face. We lie back on the bed at the same time and with nearly the same sound leaving our mouths.

This place is exhausting. They aren't exaggerating when they call this place lawless. Is this how I'm supposed to live my life? In fear?

"Are we going to talk about why you're such a good shot?" I ask.

"Nope."

"Please?"

"Not today," he says, dismissing me.

I'm starting to paint a clearer picture of Weston in my mind—a man who stays cool, calm, and collected in the middle of a gunfight. He's someone whose first thought is to protect himself and those he cares about, even if it means taking another man's life.

Who are you really?

"I'm guessing this means I'm not getting back to the Bawdy today, huh?" I ask as I wipe the blood off my hands.

"Nope." He smiles at me before closing his eyes, and I leave him to rest while I try to make some coffee.

I open the cabinet, grab a dirty metal pot, and fill it with water. I throw another piece of wood into the kitchen's fire pit. The heat from the lapping flame warms my face. I hang the pot and heat it until steam rises from it. Mixing in what looks like ground coffee creates a bitter black liquid. My lip curls in disgust. I don't think I could have made this any worse if I tried.

I walk over to Wes with a metal mug filled with the monstrosity I'm trying to pass off as coffee and place it on the table beside the bed. His snores are soft, and his hat is over his eyes. My curiosity piqued, I lift the bottom of his undershirt a bit. I bite my lip at the sight of him.

He lifts his hat and grins. "You know, if I did that, it would be considered creepy." He sits up and grabs the mug of coffee. After taking a sip, his face twists, but he swallows hard and smacks his lips together. "It's great!"

"No it's not."

"Nope, it's not. Who taught you how to make coffee?"

"Keurig," I say sarcastically.

His eyebrows pull together as he takes another sip.

"I thought you said it was terrible?" I ask.

"It is. You can't let any coffee go to waste, though."

"Let me see your leg."

Wes puts down the mug and pulls up his undershirt, exposing the wrapped wound. Blood has already seeped through the cloth, staining the bottom of his undershirt red. I carefully unwrap the fabric. It's stuck to the dried blood, and Wes bites his lip as I rip it away.

"If you weren't so pretty, I'd probably punch you in the jaw right now," he says as he blows a heavy breath from his nose.

"Aren't you a perfect gentleman." I raise my eyebrow at him.

Wes laughs and takes a deep breath. "I never said I was."

I clean the wound with more liquor, and wrap it with a new shirt. I pat it, making him wince. I trail my fingers up his thigh to pull down his undershirt, but he stops my hand and covers his lap with his arm.

"What are you doing?" He looks down at me with soft eyes and a playful smile.

I look at the firm yet gentle grasp on my wrist. Unlike any man before him, he stopped me. Wes is so different.

His free hand reaches out for me and grazes my cheek before edging behind my neck. He tugs me toward his mouth, letting his lips find mine. His kiss is hungry, and I feel just as starved.

I climb on top of his lap, and he winces as my leg touches his thigh. I kiss him and the undershirt rides up further. Without the fabric concealing him any longer, I can feel his length underneath me. We exchange heat between us, and he groans as he lifts me away from the wound on his thigh. His hands find their home at my hips. They reach behind and slide down until he's firmly gripping my ass. He growls against my neck.

"I don't think I can do this, Hannah." He breathes heavily against my mouth.

"Just let it happen," I whisper. I can't take his rejection right now. Not while the heat of his cock is against me.

"No, I mean I don't think I can do this physically." He shakes his right leg a little to remind me of his injury.

His apprehension fades as I grab the fabric of my skirt and wiggle it up over my hips. With nothing to interfere with the temptation between us, his pain seems to wash away. I drop my hips against his, and he finds his place inside me. I gasp against his neck as his groans roll over my skin. I rock my hips against his pelvis, and he thrusts into me. Heat rises through my torso and lodges itself under my diaphragm, making me tremble.

"Wes . . ." I whisper as I rock faster against him.

His thrusts hasten in response. We are perfectly in sync. Every thrust reverberates through my core, and I can feel him within the very depths of me. He grabs at my chemise strings and undoes them. The fabric spreads like butterfly wings, exposing my breasts.

"I don't mean to take the lord's name in vain, but goddamn it, Hannah. You're the most perfect woman I've ever seen."

Perfect? Not with all the scars and imperfections on my body.

He wraps his arms around me and pulls me closer into him, as if he can tell my self-doubt has crippled the motion of my hips. His tongue teases my nipples. His hand lowers and wraps around my waist so firmly it's as if I'm transferring the pleasure he gives me back into him.

He stops, and I can feel him throbbing inside of me.

"What's wrong?" I ask.

"I don't want this to end yet," he whispers against my chest.

We pull off each other's shirts and toss them to the floor. His skin gleams with sweat, and I let my fingers trace his chest. A patch of brown hair trails toward his stomach until it disappears just before his hips.

My hands graze over scarred areas on his abdomen and upper arms. Some look like healed gunshot wounds. How many times has he been shot? What stories does he keep locked inside his head? After touching the scars on his body, I touch my own. Maybe we aren't all that different, after all.

Wes thrusts again at a slow, controlled pace as he kisses me. My tongue explores his mouth, and I rock my hips on his lap. His thrusts gain speed and intensity. I can nearly feel him in my throat.

I wrap my arms around his neck, and my breasts press against his chest. Warmth radiates from our pores, and sweat drips down the arch of my back. No matter how hot we feel, it doesn't compare to the heat between our legs. The sun's rays burst through the window and radiate off our bodies. We are a synchronized entity. Sex with him is like nothing I've ever experienced. With him, I am no longer a whore.

The fire in my gut flickers wildly, burning my bones. I dig my nails into Weston's back as the flame becomes a wildfire and engulfs me entirely. I collapse against him. His thrusts become deeper and slower until he finishes as well. I lie against him and trace my fingers over his scars, trying to catch my breath.

"Seems like you've got some battle scars," I say. "Is that why you're so good with the pistol?"

"Indirectly, I suppose. My infamy with a pistol came after me and my gang robbed a post office. We were in full gallop, with four lawmen on our tails, sending a hail of gunfire right at us. I drew my pistol, leaned back, and shot the first lawman in the chest. I cocked my pistol and shot the second, who slid sideways off his horse. I shot the third in the head, and he slumped forward. I cocked the hammer again and shot a final round into the shoulder of the last lawman. He spun his horse back toward town because he knew the fight was over. I shot four men at a hoof-pounding gallop at fifty yards. It wasn't without sacrifice, though. I took a bullet above my hip. It's by the grace of god I'm even alive today." He touches the scarred areas and looks over at me.

I try to hide my shock. I knew he killed Beak and Holden, but at least those deaths had some reason behind them, even if I didn't agree with it. The killings he's just described are senseless. I draw a shaky breath.

"I'm just foolin'," he says with a smile and a laugh.

I breathe a sigh of relief, but it's short-lived.

There's a heavy knock on the door, and we struggle to get our clothes on. We walk toward the front door, still buttoning up buttons and lacing up strings. Weston opens the door, and I see the sheriff.

He looks past Weston and stares at me. "Good day, Mr. Willebrand."

"How can I help you, Sheriff?" Wes asks.

I walk over and stand on Wes's weak side. He wraps his arm around me and leans his weight on me, a smile planted on his face.

"Do you mind if I come in?"

Weston looks at me. I can see the worry on his face, but he steps aside. His movements are deliberate as he tries to avoid limping.

"Of course," Wes says. "What's this about?"

"We found two dead bandits on your road between here and town."

"Two bandits? How were they killed?" Wes feigns nervous concern.

"Gunshots," the sheriff says as he cranes his neck to try to get a glimpse of Weston's pistol. "You wouldn't know anything about that, would you?"

"Oh no. My lady and I spent the day pirooting." Weston winks at the sheriff. It's a good alibi because it definitely smells like sex and sweat in here.

The sheriff stares at me with delayed recognition and lifts his finger toward me.

"Don't you work down at the Bawdy?"

I nod, and the sheriff elbows Weston in his side.

"Weston, what are you doing bedding down with a whore in your own house?"

The word *whore* doesn't sting me. I'm immune to the bites of such degradation.

Weston clenches his jaw and offers the fakest smile I've ever seen. "I'm trying to make this one into a housewife."

"A whore will always be a whore. Bringing one home don't make it a housewife." The sheriff laughs.

Okay, that stings a bit.

"I'll try to remember that. Is there anything else we can help you with?" Wes doesn't laugh back, and the sheriff stifles his laughter.

"Nope, guess not. If you hear anything, make sure you let me know."

Weston nods and guides the Sheriff toward the door, closing it behind him. My fake smile falters, drawing into a frown. Embarrassment flushes my cheeks.

"Hannah . . ."

"No, he's right. I don't know what I was thinking. No one wants to wed a whore."

Belle's words echo in my head. Until this moment, I'd forgotten what I am.

"I wish you'd stop calling yourself that," he says. "You aren't a whore."

He wraps me up in his arms, and I hate how safe he makes me feel—how *vulnerable* he makes me feel. I didn't spend years building this wall around myself to have it torn down by *feelings*. Whores don't have feelings. We can't afford to.

I turn away from him and drop my gaze. He has no idea who I really am.

"I am, though. Don't you see? I've been bought more times than I can count. Even you paid me for my company."

"Is that what you think this is?" he says, pain in his eyes. His shoulders fall forward in defeat.

I think for a moment, and my cheeks begin to flush.

"Do you think that's *all* this is?" He repeats the question in a small and shaky voice—such a contrast to his usual confidence.

Do I think that? "That's the only reason I'm here right now, but it's not the reason I've stayed," I say with a trembling lip. Heat rises behind my eyes.

"I never paid *for* you. There was a fee to take you away from there, but it was and has always been worth every cent."

"What do you think this is, Wes?"

"I reckon it's whatever you let it be."

I can't have that responsibility. I can't *let* things be what they could be. What they should be. No matter how good Wes is for me, I can't be good enough for him.

"I'm not asking you to decide what this is right now. I'm not trying to scare you away. I know you think you're damaged, but you don't see what you do to me—the damage you've undone within *me*." He embraces me, the warmth of his body enveloping me. "You make me a better man, and I'll keep trying to show you that."

Chapter Fifteen

I'm curled up in Belle's embrace. Her arm is around my waist, and her fingers play with the fabric of my skirt. She traces her other hand along the fading bruise on my face.

I sit up and turn toward her. "If I don't tell someone, I'll go crazy."

"Tell someone what?" she asks without looking up from the pattern of my dress.

"You won't believe me because *I* hardly believe me." I let out a nervous laugh.

"Try me." Belle sits up and looks down at me with eyes the color of a summer sky.

"I'm not from here—" I begin, but she interrupts me.

"I know you aren't. You're from New York."

I exhale a deep, cleansing breath as I prepare to tell my secret. "No, Belle. I'm not from *now*. I'm from over one hundred and thirty years into the future."

Belle's hands stop moving and rest on my lap. Her eyebrows draw so close together, it makes her eyes squint. She doesn't seem surprised or shocked, as if she already knew I wasn't meant for this era. "Is that why you talk about such weird things?"

"Nothing I talk about is weird. You all are the weird ones. You can buy narcotics at the damn store. Where I'm from, empires have been created by dealing them illegally. The bathroom habits here are traumatic. The amount of rape, murder, and robberies I've seen or experienced since I've been here is unrivaled. Despite how many movies I've watched about this time period, I wasn't prepared for any of it."

Belle's eyes widen, and I can't tell if she believes me or not. Her silence is unconvincing.

"You guys think I'm above sleeping with men, but in my time, I'm an escort, which is a less threatening way to say that I sleep with men for money. I work for myself. I choose the men I sleep with off the internet. Places like the Bawdy are pretty much nonexistent in the future. Oh, and plumbing! I miss plumbing. I would give my left leg for a shower at this point, and probably my right one to get my hands on a cellphone again. And despite the exhausting amount of clothing you all wear—in the desert, I might add—I have never seen so much free balling in my life."

She stares at me as her fingers tap on the dresser, causing an uncomfortable silence between us. She draws her eyebrows together. "Cellphones and internet? I don't understand."

"I don't know how to explain these things. It's just . . . different."

Belle bites her lip. "How is sex different there?"

"For starters, we give oral like it's our job. From what I can tell, you guys don't do it very much, if ever. Here, all the men like to keep their pants on or partially on, as if it's such a hurried act. We take our time and allow every one of our senses to be awakened. The men where I'm from care a little more about us finishing, as well. Even my sleazier clients have made some attempt at making me come. I didn't, but they tried. Oh, and Belle, there are so many kinks just out in the open. Someone can have a fetish for getting peed on, and there's always one of us willing to do it. There are things like choking, whipping, and chaining. You can be straight, bi, gay, asexual, and anything in between. You can be exactly who you are without being ashamed of it. Except a pedophile. They rightfully still condemn that."

Belle smiles at me. I still don't know if she believes me or if she's just listening to me the way we listen to our clients—just nodding and looking pretty. She's definitely got the looking pretty part down.

Her leg drapes over mine as she straddles my lap, kissing me with stifled passion. "Well, if it's any consolation, I'm glad you're here."

Belle and Weston are the two redeeming parts of this place. Could I give up the luxuries of the future for my love of one or both of them? Maybe . . . but is love really enough?

I wrap my hand around the back of her head and return her kiss. I drop my hand away from her, and she pouts her lips.

"What's wrong?" she asks.

"I can't do this, Belle," I tell her, even though my body protests.

"Why not?" Belle slips off my lap and sits beside me, her features awash with rejection. Her cheeks flush red, and she can't even fake a smile.

Why not? I ask myself. "Because, Belle." I grab her face in my hand. "I love you. You're one of the main reasons I've survived here. But this place isn't for *this.*" I gesture between us. "For *us.*"

Belle is the softness that I needed to find—a source of comfort in my hardest moments. She reminded me I didn't need to be on the defense all the time. Even here. But I can't be with her. I could never be with her *because* I love her. This place wouldn't be safe for her if I slept with her. It wouldn't be safe for either of us.

Besides, my heart still thumps to a confused rhythm, pulling closer to Wes with every contraction of the muscle. I'm not sure if it should be. I'm not sure that he should course through my fibers. He's a man, and men do nothing but leave with a part of me, even when giving myself freely.

But Wes didn't steal anything from inside me. If anything, he put a little something back.

"Belle . . ." I reach for her hand, but she pulls away and stands up. She isn't mad. She looks small and broken instead, as if the soft touch of my rejection was just hard enough to make her shatter.

"I understand, Hannah. I do." Belle backs against my dresser. She turns toward it, rustling coins beneath her trembling fingers.

I look away from her, dropping my gaze in guilt. I never wanted to hurt her.

"This place isn't for me, or you, or us. We're whores." She turns back toward me, beckoning my gaze with nothing more than her tone. "I want you to get out of here. I want you to do what I can't. You need to leave with that rancher. Let him take you away from this hell."

"I can't leave you," I whisper.

"Yes, you can. You have to."

"I won't!"

She walks over and wraps me in a tight embrace. She pulls away and holds me at arm's length. Her cerulean eyes are glassy. A single tear falls down her cheek and hovers on the rosy curve of her lower lip. "I love you, Hannah. I need you to promise me you'll leave. Go with that man. Be happy. Let your body be your own again. Mine will never be."

"I can't promise you that. I can't. I won't leave while you're still stuck here."

"My soul will be stuck in this wretched place forever. You have to stop trying to free something meant to be trapped. I'm a caged bird, unwilling to leave the confines of this cage. But you're something that can't be contained. Not here or anywhere."

She kisses my lips once more, and the salt of her tear reaches my tongue. She brushes my hair back and smiles, looking at me one more time before leaving my bedroom. My door clicks shut behind her, feeling ominously final. I hear her door open and close as I lie back on the bed and smooth my skirt over my hips.

I look up at the ceiling. It's crumbling in on itself, too heavy with secrets. My heart beats between my ears, reminding me that it's awakened. Maybe Belle is right. I should leave this life behind. But to leave means to abandon her . . . and my chance of ever going home.

Weston's ranch can never be my *home*. I want to love him, but I'm not entirely sure how. Just the thought of loving a man makes my palms hot with sweat. My body tenses, remembering the touch of so many hands before his. I wish I didn't have to fight to feel. I wish I wasn't too afraid to let myself be loved.

To numb myself and my excitable heartbeat, I open the dresser drawer and dig for the bottle of laudanum. I push clothes aside but find nothing but fabric. I don't remember taking it out since the last time Belle and I used it.

Belle.

I open the door of my room and look down the hallway. Seeing no sign of the madam, I cross into Belle's room. No candles or lamps illuminate the darkness. My foot brushes against something that sounds like glass as I spot Belle's silhouette on the bed. I light the lamp on the table next to the bed and look down at the floor. I'd kicked over the bottle of laudanum. The escaped liquid spreads its fingers across the floorboards and reaches out as far as it can go before seeping through the fibers of the wood.

"Belle?" I whisper into the silence. There's no response. It's so quiet, I can hear the lamp's flame flickering and lashing at the glass. I light a candle and bring it toward the bed.

Belle is sprawled out with her arms on either side of her, palms up. Her fingers are slightly curled, and her chest is motionless. With unsteady legs, I put the candle on the table and wrap her up in my arms. Her skin is still warm.

"No, Belle . . . why?"

She takes a shallow breath. I cradle her and rock her body as I look down at her lips. Moments ago, they had been on my own. She draws another shallow breath, but there's too much time between them. I fight the urge to call for help. Nothing can be done. There's nothing here to help her. Would she even want help if there were? I hold my breath as I wait for her chest to rise again. It's still.

I plead for a breath to rush past her pale lips, but when I put my head to her chest, I hear only silence. I touch the side of her neck and try to feel for a pulse. I think I feel one, but I realize it's my own panicked heartbeat causing vibrations within my fingertips.

My heart sinks. She took her life with the laudanum I purchased. The drug seeped through her and wrapped its hands around her throat. I can no longer drown within her blue eyes because they're closed, as if she is merely sleeping.

I take solace in knowing she didn't feel pain in her final moments. The drug would have numbed the physical and mental anguish. She would have felt nothingness—a feeling she had been chasing. I imagine her joy once she escaped this life and floated above her body—the dreaded vessel that endured such unspeakable abuse. I cope with the pain ripping through my heart by reminding myself that she's free now.

I kiss her cheek for the last time. "I will miss you as long as there is breath within my lungs, Belle," I whisper.

I walk into the hall with a dizzying headache and yell for help. A wave of bright dresses runs toward Belle's room, pushing me out of the way. The madam gasps and the hallway fills with murmurs as the other women try to push past each other to see Belle in her most compromised state.

Ivy walks over to me with pursed lips. "You shouldn't be crying, firefly. Belle was destined for the bottle."

"What?" I look up at her and wipe tears from my eyes.

"Girls like her don't survive long here. Too soft. Fragile," Ivy says with a cruel smile as she cocks her hip. "She lasted longer than I expected, I suppose."

Belle might have been soft, but she was also strong enough to end her own life when it no longer suited her. With half a beat missing from every thump of my heart, my stomach twists into a knot as a revelation washes over me.

Belle freed herself to set me free.

CHAPTER SIXTEEN

I stand on the doorstep of the Bawdy, smoking a cigarette without coughing because my lungs have become accustomed to the strong tobacco. The embers sizzle, and I exhale the thick smoke into the warm, stagnant air above my head.

Wes rides to the front of the Bawdy around his usual time, and I look up at him and smile through tight lips. He frowns as he dismounts and walks over to me.

"What's wrong?" he asks as he touches my face.

"My friend died." I say this casually, with no more tears left to cry.

"I'm so sorry." He wraps his strong arms around me, and I lean into him as I exhale a final drag of the cigarette. "I wanted to take you on a little road trip, but I'd understand if you didn't want to go now."

I look back at the Bawdy and shiver before turning back to Wes and nodding at him. "Where are we going?"

"Just to the next town over."

Wes brushes his hand through his hair before mounting Concetta and reaching his hand down for me. Once I wrap my arms around him, he takes off in the opposite direction of his home. Excitement fills me at the thought of being any place but here.

We ride for a while, and my throat grows dry and scratchy. I tap on his shoulder. "I'm thirsty. We've been riding for what feels like forever," I whine.

"We're nearly there. Just a few more minutes." He glances back at me.

We arrive in the town of Harlow, which is much more established than Sundown. The saloon has a sign instead of words painted on the building, and the vibe is more welcoming than that of the Bawdy.

Why couldn't I have been dumped into this place instead?

I slide off Concetta's back, drawn to the doors of the saloon by my desire for a drink. Wes jumps down, hitches the horse to a post, and follows after me.

"Don't just walk in there yourself," he says. "Stay by me." He looks at me with furrowed brows.

The moment the doors close behind us, the patrons eye us with mistrust. Wes locks his arm in mine protectively, and we walk toward the bar. The bartender raises an eyebrow in suspicion.

"Is this how y'all treat visitors?" Wes says. "How about asking what we'd like to drink?"

"We just know who you are, mister, and we don't want no trouble." The elderly bartender raises his hands.

"No trouble at all." Wes smiles, and I look up at him.

The bartender lowers his hands slowly. "If that's the case, what can I get you two?"

"Two beers." Wes leans back against the bar and looks around the saloon.

I follow suit.

The loud and upbeat music thumps in my chest. Men play poker in the corner. Two of them kick their chairs back and begin to yell at each other over a foul hand. The madam here runs over to get between them. The women work the floor, handling the men with the confidence I once had. Coins are passed to them every few minutes, and their hips wiggle sensually as they disappear around the back of the saloon with clients.

The bartender slides two glasses of beer toward us, and we pick our drinks up. I gulp it down, trying to rehydrate my tired body.

"That whore sure can drink," the bartender says with a grin.

Wes tenses as if he might leap over the bar. I grab his arm and pull him toward me, rubbing his wrist and mouthing, *it's fine*.

"This *whore* would like another beer, please," I say. The moment the beer is placed beside me, I grab it and begin to sip at the bitter brown drink. "Why are we here, anyway?" I ask with a cock of my head.

"I'm riding in a competition tomorrow," he says, looking around the saloon with an alert gaze.

"Riding what?"

"A bull." He smiles at me.

"You are not!" I drop my glass on the table too hard, and the noise has everyone in the room turning to look. My cheeks flush as a wave of insecurity washes over me.

"Oh, I am. There's a nice prize pool. I'll get money as long as I can make at least fourth place."

I look out the window and see the sun setting in the sky, bursting with oranges and reds. "Where are we staying?"

"Here." He turns toward the bartender. "I can rent a room here, right?"

"I don't know. We're pretty full because of the—"

Wes cuts him off by pulling some bills out of his pocket

and passing them across the table. It's a higher amount than the room is worth.

The bartender stares at him, curls his lip, and hands him a metal key on a chain. "You can have room three."

"Thank you for your hospitality." His words are laced with sarcasm.

Wes locks his arm into mine, and we walk toward the hotel rooms behind the saloon. He wiggles the handle as the key sticks in the lock, cursing under his breath. When the door finally swings open, the musty smells of old hotel room and sex hang in the air. I flop onto the bed, too tired to care. Every muscle in my body aches, and I rub them to try to soothe them. The room is similar to the one at the Bawdy, but cleaner and more modern.

Modern? Can anything really be considered that here?

Wes shrugs out of his jacket and places it on the dresser before pulling off his day shirt. With a smirk creeping across my face, my mind wanders at the sight of his rippling muscles. The memory of his strong body on top of mine makes me ache between my legs. His belt rattles as he unfastens it and places it on top of his jacket. He dives into bed with me, very ungracefully. He places his hat on the table beside the bed and smiles at me.

"Your turn," he says as his fingers graze the fabric of my chemise. His touch ignites my skin, and goosebumps rise in its path.

"I'm taking my skirt off, but I'm going to bed," I tell him with a yawn.

"Fine." The corners of his lips turn downward.

I wiggle out of my skirt, throw it beside the bed, and curl up against his chest, wearing only my chemise. The bed's scratchy fabric claws at my bare skin. "Why can't we stay here and leave Sundown behind?" I ask.

"I can't stay in this town for . . . reasons." He rubs his

hand through his hair nervously. He's lucky I'm too tired to press further.

"I have to tell you something," I say, avoiding his gaze.

Wes sits up on his elbow and stares at me. "Okay, shoot."

"I had feelings for the girl who died at the Bawdy." As soon as the words leave my lips, the anxiety causes my stomach to twist. It's not that I meant to hide it from him. We just never had a chance to talk about it.

"Oh," he says.

"Are you mad?"

Wes laughs. "About a woman, Hannah? No. I'm mad about every other man that's ever been inside you, but not that. I reckon life's too short to get worked up about such a thing." He brushes my hair from my face. "I'm sorry about your friend."

"Me too."

His hand traces along my side. His fingertips graze my skin. The effects of the strong beer amplify the sensations. The rough skin of his fingers reaches the outside of my thigh —down and back up—until I'm shivering at his touch. My eyes flutter as they grow heavy, and his soothing caress helps me fall into the deepest sleep I've had since I've gotten here.

THE SALOON DOORS SLAM BEHIND US AS WE WALK outside and take in the fresh air of the morning. People meander about with excitement over the competition. They've been drawn from all over the surrounding areas. Some look incredibly fancy and well dressed.

When we reach the arena, Wes drags me over toward an open area of the fence, and I lean against it.

"I'll be back," he says. "Hopefully." He laughs, and I smack his chest.

A large paddock has been set up in the middle of town, just for this event. I catch a glimpse of several muscular beasts on the far side of the fence. Their horns protrude from their heads. The tips have been sawed off a bit, but they're still dangerous. The animals snort as a man walks to the center of the arena and speaks with a booming voice.

"Welcome to the fifth annual bull riding competition. Prizes are given for the best rides for the top four contestants. These bulls are hot and ready."

Applause rises from the crowd, and my lips tighten. *If something happens to him, do they even have real doctors here?* I look around and see a painted sign above a tent that says Doctor, with a man asleep beneath it. *Great.*

I watch as the men are thrown, one after another. The bulls run past in a blaze of fury. Several men manage to stay on the bulls, but the man before Wes gets dragged out, clutching a bleeding wound in his abdomen. A deep red stain spreads across the rider's dirty shirt. The fabric has a tear in it, exposing the frayed flesh. Another man rips the shirt the rest of the way, shoving it against the rider's stomach to hold pressure on it.

I try to catch Wes's gaze from across the fence, but it's too late. He's already preparing for his ride on top of a huge black bull. My heart races. I want to jump up and scream for him to stop. The crowd roars with excitement, ripping away the opportunity to call to him.

The animal's giant muscles twitch, and his nares flare in anger. Sweat drips from my forehead. I try to excuse myself through the crowd to find someone to stop the ride before it begins. Angry voices pipe up from behind me as I shimmy through their hot bodies. The scent of wood, body odor, and overly strong perfume overpower me.

The announcer's muffled voice rises above the crowd, and my shoulders fall forward. I'm too late.

A man in a cowboy hat slides open the wooden gate, and the bull takes off toward the center of the paddock. Wes jerks back and forth as the beast bucks and twists in the air.

My eyes widen as the bell chimes. He jumps down from the bull, and it charges, head low and horns poised. Wes dives, rolls, and jumps up before he runs toward the gate. His hands reach up to his head, and he smirks at me as he runs back into the midst of the paddock where the bull snorts hot breath toward him. He grabs his hat, places it on his head, and jogs out of the arena.

He runs up to me, panting and breathless, with a smile on his face. "How was that?" he asks.

"Impressive," I say, and I mean it. There was something primordial about the way he handled the animal. "What happens now?"

Wes drags his arm across his forehead to wipe away the sweat, leaving a streak of dirt in its place. "We wait for the results. They usually do a little show in the ring. We can stick around and watch it if you want."

I wrinkle my nose and shake my head. After seeing what the future has to offer, it'll be difficult for a dinky little sideshow from the 1880s to hold my attention. He nods and presses his palm against my lower back, guiding me through the crowd.

We walk around for a bit, admiring the bulls and cattle in the holding pens. There's a horse auction happening in a stall a little ways away from the main event. We wander over and watch. None are as well-muscled or beautiful as Concetta or Hickock. These stringy animals, with their sunken and sad eyes, make me realize just how much Wes cares for his mounts. It stirs up pride in my heart.

As if sensing my discomfort at seeing the state of the

horses, he leads me back toward the main arena. "I snagged Concetta from an auction like this one. She was in worse shape than those nags, if you can believe it," he says.

"It must have taken a lot of work to get her looking like she does now."

He nods. "I saw something in her. She was dirty and tired and hated every man that came near her, but she was beautiful to me. All it took was a little kindness and patience."

I can't help but wonder if he's talking about Concetta or me. Before I can ask, the announcer takes the center of the arena and quiets the crowd. I look at Wes, but he doesn't meet my gaze.

"The results are in, ladies and gents. Our judges had a hard time agreeing on fourth place, so we'll start there."

I hold my breath.

"Fourth place is Weston Willebrand," the man says. "Great ride."

Wes's attention snaps toward the announcer, and a smile creeps across his face. He grabs my shoulders with excitement, and I smile back at him, despite finding this idea ludicrous and dangerous.

"I'll collect the prize and we'll get going, okay?"

I nod at him. He walks up to the announcer and receives a stack of bills. He waves at the crowd before walking back to me.

A drunk man grabs at my arm and tugs me, pulling me into him. He grinds his crotch against my body as he exhales a hot breath in my ear. "How much?" he whispers.

I shove my elbow back and make contact with his nose. The man fumbles and clutches his face, looking wildly at Wes.

"This bitch just—"

Wes smiles at me with pride, draws back his arm, and

socks the man in the face again. The man falls to the ground in front of him.

"This *bitch* is mine," he says toward the unconscious man. His lips tighten, and he shakes out his hand. He looks back at me with a hint of sadness and hands me a portion of the money. "Guess it's time to get you back to the Bawdy, Hannah."

I shake my head and look into his rich brown eyes as the decision forms in my gut and erupts from my mouth. "I'm not going back to the Bawdy."

Chapter Seventeen

One arm is around Weston's waist, and the other rests on my thigh as we trot toward his farm, passing the sad town of Sundown on our right. When we arrive at the fork in the road, Concetta slows to a walk, and Wes cranes his head to glance behind me at the rider who just rode past. The other man eyes us as well. Weston looks ahead, as if ignoring the situation will make it go away.

The man turns his horse around and rides up beside us. "Marshall! I thought that was you!" the stranger says as he points to Wes.

Weston keeps his gaze on the horizon in front of him. "I think you might have mistaken me for someone else."

"No, I think not. You're Marshall Williams. The infamous Maw. We thought you'd died."

Wes turns his head to look at the man beside us. His eyes lock on with a fierceness that unnerves me. I remove my arm from his waist and rest it on my hip. There are times when I don't even know who Wes is. He morphs into an aggressive, gruff, and reckless person. Maybe he is this "Marshall."

"I said, you have the wrong person. Now get going." His words are clipped and harsh. They lash from his tongue and into the air between the two men.

The stranger's lips become tight and thin. He squints his eyes, even though the sun is behind us. "Have it your way." He turns his horse around, and they canter off toward town.

Weston finally takes a deep breath. By the time we reach his farm, he's soaked in sweat. His back is moist through his jacket. I've never seen Weston afraid—and he still isn't—but something about that stranger has him rattled.

He dismounts, helps me down, and releases Concetta into her pen. When we walk inside his house, he starts searching for something.

"What are you looking for?" I ask.

His eyes dart around the room. "Nothing," he says with a strained voice as he looks under the bed and pulls out a lever-action rifle.

"Should I be worried?"

"No." He checks the chamber to see if it's loaded and sets it next to his bed.

He's being very short with me, and that isn't like him. I grab his arm, but he sidesteps out of my grasp. With a sigh, he sits on the bed.

"Wes . . ."

"I shouldn't have brought you here." He drops his head into his hands.

"Why? What's wrong?"

"I haven't been completely honest with you."

Honesty? That's one thing this relationship has been lacking from the very beginning. I'm not honest with him, down to the most intimate fiber of my being. There's nothing truthful about me here, except for my profession. My name isn't even Hannah—the most basic lie I didn't even need to tell.

"What do you mean?"

"I was part of a group called the Shiloh Gang." Weston's eyes fixate as he descends deep into a memory. "It was me, Elias, Gil, and Chet. Elias was our leader. Gil and Chet were fools, but they were like brothers to me." Wes drops his gaze. "We robbed anything on wheels. Train cars, stagecoaches, wagons . . . you name it.

"Things started to go south when Elias had a couple tied up in the back of a stagecoach. While Chet and Gil were loading up our haul, Elias . . . killed the husband. He told me to shoot the wife, but I couldn't bring myself to do it." He took a deep breath. "Elias said we had to do it. He said when you get sympathetic, you get sloppy. When you get sloppy, you get caught. I holstered my pistol and hopped down from the coach. I heard the gunshot and then nothing. It was never the same after that."

"How many people did you rob?" I ask him, though I'm not sure I want to know the answer.

"A lot. So many that there's no way I don't have a first-class seat right next to the devil himself."

"So who was that guy back on the road?"

"Gil. We made off with a lock box full of jewelry at one of our last stagecoach robberies. We were supposed to split it four ways, but it disappeared. I heard Gil's been looking for me because he thinks I took it."

"Did you?"

He looks at me with no emotion on his face. "No, I think Elias took it, but he's dead. If he did take the jewelry, its whereabouts are buried with him."

"Is this actually your family farm?"

"No. I found it abandoned." His gaze falls to the floor, and he plays with the brim of his hat. He and I both know this is a lie. I assume the desperation of running from the law and his own gang drove him to commandeer this farm and steal the owner's identity. Whoever Weston Willebrand was, he's not the man sitting beside me.

"Were you even married?" My pitch is higher than I intended it to be, surprise rippling through me over just how much Wes isn't who he says he is.

"Yes, that part's true."

I wish I could tell him my truths, but he would never believe me. I can believe his stories since I've seen the surety of his finger on the trigger. He is Marshall. But he's also Wes. He's two people, fused together and stitched with brutality.

I ball up my hands in my lap to stop them from trembling. Deep in my heart, Wes is everything I knew he was. He was a gang member, and it sounds like he was quite the good one at that. I drop my gaze, and he reaches his arm out to grab my shoulder.

I shrug out of his grasp and scoot away from him. "I don't even know who you are. How could you do all those things?"

"It was a different time. A different me. We did whatever we had to do to keep from hanging tight from the gallows."

Did he though? How can I love someone so brazen and dark?

He leans into me and kisses me, yanking me away from my thoughts. I lose the battle against him at the taste of his lips. He twirls the strings of my chemise around his finger.

"You know . . . I'm not hurt anymore." He smirks against my mouth.

"What should I even call you? Weston or Marshall?"

"Wes," he says as he stands up, strips off his jacket, and pulls his undershirt over his head. The candlelight dances off his chest. He unbuttons his pants, and the fabric splays open, exposing him fully. "Let me show you the man you've made me, Hannah."

He leans over my body and places his lips against mine.

There's hesitation in my kiss, and he notices. He pulls away from me.

"What's wrong?" His hand brushes through my hair, tucking it behind my ear.

What's wrong? *Everything* is wrong. The time, the place, and maybe even the person. I hate how right it feels when he touches me, as his hand snakes around the back of my neck. How the twitch of his cock beckons me. The way his heart thumps in tune with mine as his body is pressed against me. I feel so safe beneath him—sheltered from all the things I fear.

"Nothing," I say with a tight-lipped smile as I untie my chemise.

He growls against the skin of my collarbone. I wiggle out of my skirt and throw it next to the bed as Weston's hungry hands explore the curves of my ass and the arches of my breasts. I wrap my legs around his waist and feel the heat of him as he leans over me. He draws the strength and tenacity in his grasp from Marshall, the gentleness in his kiss from Wes. If I want to be with him, I have to accept that this is a troubled threesome.

I rub my hand through his thick brown hair, and he looks down at me with hickory-brown eyes. He kisses me with passion and drives himself inside me. I gasp at his size and strength when he's over me, allowing his deep and greedy thrusts. I feel small and safe under him, as if his body will shield me from anything malevolent. My anxious thoughts melt into the crook of his arm beneath me and absorb into his skin.

"Oh, Hannah," he groans into my neck as I dig my nails into his sides and pull him in deeper with my legs. Wes grabs my wrists and pins them above my head. His thrusts are hungry, as if he can't be deep enough within me.

My moans pierce the silence of the room.

He's different from any other man I've met, both in this era and my own. His body becomes one with mine, altering my perspective on sex. He makes me question my own reality.

"Let me turn over," I say.

He pulls out so I can reposition onto my belly. My breasts press against the mattress as I lift my hips and spread my legs. His hands race along the arch of my back with excited fingertips. He reaches down and grips himself before taking a deep breath and exhaling slowly.

"Is everything okay?" I ask him. I can't help but wonder if I did something wrong.

"Just the sight of you right now is enough to end this far too soon."

I pull my legs back together and drop onto my side as he lies beside me and wraps his arm around my waist.

"I'm sorry. Just give me a minute," he whispers, and wipes the sweat off his forehead as beads of it drip down the molded muscles of his chest. Manual labor does his body justice.

I kiss him and reach down to tease him with my fingers.

He groans against my mouth. "You aren't helping."

"Do you want me to get dressed?"

"No!" He nearly snarls the word as he sits up on his knees. He grabs me and rolls me back onto my stomach.

I lift my hips to meet his, and he surges within me. His groan is otherworldly as he finds the farthest depths of me. His thrusts are deep and slow as his hands grip my hips. He slams into me, and the sound of our bodies resonates into the stale silence.

"Grab my hair," I whisper.

"No, I don't want to hurt you," he says with a groan.

"You won't. Just do it, Wes."

After a moment of hesitation, he reaches out his arm and grabs a fistful of my hair.

"Pull harder," I command.

He draws his arm backward, and the tension cranes my head back. I close my eyes. The pain electrifies my scalp and sends currents through my brain, causing me to moan loudly. He pulls harder, forcing me to lift my body toward him. He wraps his other arm around my waist and reaches up to fill his hand with my breast. He squeezes, and I bite my lip. His thrusts quicken until a fire erupts inside me. Instead of beginning as a small flame and gaining strength, it emerges from the start as a blaze. The flames lash at the inside of my pelvis and up through my belly, engulfing me. I shudder against him. His groan rolls over my moan, and my fire ignites him as well.

He throbs inside me as we collapse. The pulsations send ripples through my pelvis, and we fall asleep, entwined and smoldering.

Chapter Eighteen

I wake up and yawn. The sun has already risen into the crisp blue sky, and its heat radiates off the sand, creating a mirage outside. Wes snores softly beside me. I bite my lip and trace my fingers up his thigh, and he stiffens at my touch.

"What are you doing, miss?" He finally opens his eyes as I slip between his legs. "What are you—" His words cut off, and his voice fades into a groan. His fingers grip the mattress as I take every inch of him into my mouth. "Hannah," he half whispers and half groans my name. He drops his head back and begins to thrust his hips upward, pushing himself deeper into my mouth.

My hand reaches up and slides across the brown hair above his pelvis, my mouth keeping in sync with his movements.

"Hannah, I'm going to . . ."

I push him to the back of my throat and feel him release. I crawl up to him, wipe my mouth, and lie beside him again.

"Where the hell are you from, and what was that?" Wes

brushes the hair from my face and speaks with an intoxicated whisper.

"That, my dear, sweet Wes, was the best blowjob you'll ever get."

"Blowjob?" He cocks his head.

I roll my eyes. "I fellated you!"

He wraps his arms around me and kisses my forehead. "I'm glad you decided not to go back to the Bawdy."

"There's nothing there for me anymore." The pain in my heart reemerges at the thought of Belle.

I imagine her lifeless body being removed from her bedroom as the madam merely worries about how to make up the lost income. That's all we are to her.

He pulls me into his chest and hugs me so tight that it draws the unbearable sadness from my heart. "What happened?"

"She committed suicide with laudanum." I stare ahead, the memory plaguing me.

"That's the prostitute's drink of choice for that." He sucks his teeth.

"Don't call her that! Did you forget where I'm from?" I shoot daggers at him with my eyes.

"But you're different."

"So was she."

He lifts his hand to try and touch my face, but I recoil from him. He wisely shuts up before he digs his hole any deeper.

Wood creaks outside, and we look out the window. Despite not seeing anything, Wes remains tense. He stands up and grabs the rifle, cocking the lever as he walks toward the front door. He opens it, and his heavy steps fall along the porch. After coming back inside, he walks around the house with the rifle clutched against his chest until calming down enough to let the barrel fall to his side.

"What has you so worked up?" I ask.

"Nothing."

"I would prefer it if you didn't lie to me. Nothingness doesn't cause this." I gesture toward him—nude, barefoot, and having just walked around on the porch with a rifle.

With a deflated breath, Wes sits down beside me. "Remember when I told you Gil's been looking for me? He knows where I live now. There's only one farm on this road."

My eyebrows furrow. "So?"

"He'll be coming for me, Hannah. I'll never forgive myself if you become collateral damage for something that has nothing to do with you. All because of me."

"He'd hurt me?"

"Oh yes. He'll harm who I care about most if it'll force a confession out of me." Wes drops his gaze and wrings his hands on the barrel of the rifle.

"But you don't have the—"

"He doesn't know that! He's going to hurt you until he does, though."

"What are we going to do?"

"There's nothing we can do, and there's nowhere to go. The safest place for you would be back at the Bawdy." He stands up, throws my clothes at me, and steps into his pants.

"I'm not going back there." I toss the skirt off my lap and stare at him.

"Please . . ." he pleads.

"I'm staying with you."

Wes stares at the skirt on the floor, as if his head and his heart are locked in a battle of wills. "Well, come on then. At least let me teach you to shoot."

We get dressed, and I wear another of Mary's split skirts. We walk toward the back of the house next to the barn, and Wes sets up some bottles on top of a hitching post. He draws his pistol from its holster and loads six bullets.

"You have to cock it every time before you shoot again," he says. "The cylinder will rotate until you run out of bullets. Grip it here, and aim the barrel down range." He places my hand around the grip and adjusts my fingers, his body pressed into me.

I cock the pistol, pull the trigger, and instinctively close my eyes at the sound. Birds rise from the sand in retreat. I missed every bottle, so I cock the gun and fire again. Another miss. He nudges me closer to the bottles and has me shoot again. I hit the green glass bottle, and it shatters in the air. Shards fall onto the sand below.

"Well," he says, "I guess we just have to get you real close so you can't miss."

He laughs, takes the pistol from me, and walks until he's almost flush with the house, tripling the length between himself and the hitching post. He cocks the revolver and fires. The brown bottle next to the one I shot breaks and falls to the ground. He shoots the second and third bottle so fast, I can hardly tell he's cocked the hammer.

"Can you put up another set of bottles?" he yells toward me, and I oblige.

I place three more glass bottles on top of the hitching post. They wiggle slightly, and it's hard to get them to sit still. Once I step out of the way, he picks up his lever action rifle and raises it to his cheek, looking down the sights. He cocks the hammer and pulls the trigger. He takes out all three bottles in quick succession.

There's a tingling between my legs while watching him shoot. Seeing his arms flex as he handles the weapon causes unexpected feelings of excitement. But also a pang of guilt because of the innocent people that were on the other side of his barrel at one point.

Wes walks over and tosses a folding knife from his pocket

into my hands. "I had another one, but I don't know where it went."

I bite the inside of my cheeks as I remember I left his knife at the Bawdy. I meant to return it. I take the knife and slip it into my pocket. Wes lifts his hat and wipes sweat from his brow, his hair damp with perspiration. I look down at my arms, marred with dirt and wind-blown sand from our shooting lesson.

"I don't think I'm going to like the answer, but do you have anywhere to take a bath here?"

"I do."

I can't hide the disbelief and joy on my face. "Where?"

He leads me into the barn. A cow with a calf bellows and sticks its wet nose out to nudge me. A few goats stand up on their hind legs, watching me with curious, dark eyes. At the back of the barn, I see what looks like a watering trough for animals. It shimmers with sunlight from the window above. The water inside is tinged brown from some rust on the sides, and a few tiny pieces of hay float on the surface. I reach my hand in, and soothing heat surrounds my skin.

"How is it so warm?"

"The sun does all the work. At least the heat here is good for one thing."

"Mind if I take a quick bath?"

Before he can answer, I begin stripping off my clothes, and Wes eyes me with equal excitement. My toes test the water before I let myself drop into it. He hands me a black block like what was in the washtub, and he leaves me alone in the barn.

Suds build in the water as I wash myself. I dunk my head under and clean my hair for the first time since I arrived in 1885. I feel as if I've won the lottery, and my prize was an old watering trough filled with warm, stagnant water. I never got a chance to take more than a sponge bath at the Bawdy, and being able to clean under my armpits and between my legs makes me feel human again.

Droplets of water slip from my clavicle, down my chest, and drip off my nipples as I stand. I step out of the tub and lean over to ring out my hair. A hand covers my mouth. I grasp at the pale wrist—most definitely not Wes's tanned skin—and dig my nails into it.

"Fucking bitch," the voice says from behind me through clenched teeth.

He loosens his hold on my mouth enough for me to let out the start of a scream, but he grabs me again. I struggle against him, the smell of body odor wafting over me as he presses his weight against my naked body. I know where this is going. Just when I started to feel like a person again.

He cocks a pistol and puts the barrel to my head. The cold metal presses against my temple. "If you stop screaming, I'll let you get dressed. Okay?"

I nod against his hand, and he removes it from my mouth. He steps back, keeping the barrel of his pistol pointed at me. I recognize him as the man from yesterday—Gil.

"Can you look away?" I ask, my cheeks flushing.

"No. If I can't touch, the least I can do is watch."

I'm glad he won't touch me, but I wonder if it's because he can't get it up or if he won't because of Wes. I stare at him while I dress. As I slip on my shoes, he walks toward me. Red hair peeks out from under his dingy hat, and his lifeless green eyes roam over my figure.

"Has Marshall said anything about any jewelry?"

"No," I tell him quickly. Maybe too quickly.

He punches me in the face, and I fall to the ground beside the tub. I grip the metal and try to pull myself up, but he lifts his boot and kicks me in the gut. My ribs explode with pain.

"He said Elias probably has the jewelry," I say in a quiet and strained voice.

He grabs me by my hair and lifts me to my feet. "Elias is dead," he whispers back. "He ain't got it. I didn't even have to touch him. I just tortured his wife, and the old coot died of a heart attack. If he had it, he would have told me before I let her bleed out."

My stomach sinks, and I gag. Wes is right. Gil will kill me before he's satisfied with Weston's answer, and I'm not even sure Wes cares about me enough to make me the proper pawn in Gil's game.

"Gil, you have it all wrong. I'm just a prostitute here with Wes . . . Marshall. I'm not the person to use as bait. He isn't going to care about me enough to give up the jewelry, even if he does have it." The words spill from my mouth in a flurry.

Gil hesitates for a moment before punching me in the face again. Blood drips from my nose and falls onto my white shirt.

"We'll see about that," he says. "Men don't usually bring a whore home." He says *whore* with such disdain on his lips.

He's not buying my lie, so I try a different approach. "He's the best shot here. You should really get out of here before he sees what you've done."

"I thought you might say that." He lifts his coat and drops Wes's rifle and pistol onto the ground. "He made it so easy. He left the guns by the house when he brought you in here." He laughs and kicks the guns, sending them skittering toward the wall. "Go ahead. Yell for him."

"No," I say with a shake of my head, unwilling to call Wes into a trap.

He punches me in the side of my head, and I fall to the floor again. I curl up as I try to defend myself from another kick. An unintentional scream leaves the depths of my throat as his boot stomps the side of my chest.

"Hannah?" Wes yells from somewhere outside the barn.

I try to tell him to keep away, but my voice comes out in a gurgled whisper as the blood from my nose floods my throat. The barn door bursts open.

"Hannah!" Wes tries to walk toward me.

"Don't come any closer!" Gil shouts, raising his gun.

"Wes . . . don't," I sputter, the pain cutting off my words.

Wes is visibly shaking. He looks down at his guns behind Gil's legs. He must feel so naked without his weapons.

"Marshall. Where's the jewelry?"

Wes rubs his jaw, his eyes wide. "I don't have it!"

"Well, Elias doesn't have it either. I made sure of that."

"What about Chet?"

"Lucky for you, I found you first. Spotted you out on the road, and you didn't even have the decency to ask me how I've been. And after all we've been through, Marshall."

Wes lifts his hands defensively, taking almost imperceptible steps closer to us. "Just don't hurt her. She has nothing to do with this." He looks at me. "Are you okay?"

"Thank you for asking," Gil answers instead. "I've been doing terrible!" He tosses his head back with a humorless laugh. "I've been homeless for the last year. I sleep in the fucking desert. Yet here I find you on this great little farm, living a grand ol' life. How'd you get this place? Killed the owner?"

"I found it."

"Sure you did. The infamous Maw is a killer. He'll always be a killer." He turns toward me and leans down. "Do you know how many people he's killed?"

I shake my head.

"Your fella here has killed better than twenty people over the course of two years. Anyone who saw our faces. He'd kill a dog if it had gotten a look at us."

149

I look up at Wes. He doesn't even try to defend himself. His shoulders fall forward, and I know Gil speaks the truth.

"He even raped some of the women we tied up," Gil continues.

"I never raped anyone, Gil, and you know that!" Wes shouts. "That was you and Chet who enjoyed making the women suffer before killing them! I didn't get fucking pleasure from what I did."

I want to believe what Wes is saying. I don't think he was a rapist. But then again, I didn't realize he was such a killer.

"Are you going to tell me where the jewelry is?" Gil prods one more time, jutting the barrel of his gun toward Wes.

"I don't know!" Wes screams back, his voice strained.

Gil pulls me onto my knees and brandishes a knife. The sun reflects off the metal as he brings the blade toward the soft skin of my throat.

"No! Don't!" Wes's eyes dart between Gill and me.

"Where's the jewelry?" Gil demands.

"I don't have it!"

Gil makes a shallow slice in the front of my neck. The pain is hardly noticeable compared to the rest of the pain in my face and ribs, but I can feel a trickle of blood slide toward my chest.

"Why don't you come fight me like a man, Gil?"

"I don't need to fight you." Gil shoots Wes a yellow-toothed smile.

"Don't you? Remember Marlene?" Wes's face twists into an expression I haven't seen. Maniacal almost.

"My wife?"

"Oh yeah, she was incredible!" Wes grabs his crotch and does a thrust into his hand.

"You fucked my wife?" Gil nearly drops his pistol at this.

"Several times."

"You fucking piece of shit!"

Gil holsters his pistol and walks toward Wes with heavy and determined steps. He swings at him, but Weston dodges his fist. They embrace each other, locked in a grapple. Gil tries to swing into Wes's jaw, but Wes leans his head back, dodging the blow. Wes takes the opportunity to lay a hard punch on Gil's side, sending him stumbling backward. Shaking it off, Gil crouches and spears his body into Weston, causing them both to fall to the ground. Gil draws his elbow back and punches Wes in the face again, sending blood spraying from Wes's mouth. Wes tries to block the punches the best he can, but he's in a terrible position.

Wes finally speaks up. "Gil, I fucking saved you!"

He lifts his hip and rolls Gil onto his back. In a swift motion, he lays a hard blow on Gil's cheek. Blood shines slick and red on their skin and makes it harder for the men to grab each other. Gil flips Wes onto his back again, grabs his head, and slams it into the floor, knocking him out.

I cover my mouth to stifle a scream as the sounds of fists on flesh permeate the barn. Through my glassy vision, I catch sight of the pistol in the corner. I will my legs to make a run for the gun—to do what Wes taught me—but I'm frozen in place. I'm not sure if it's fear or if the confession about Wes has iced my feet to the ground.

Gil stands up and stumbles toward me, grabbing a fistful of my hair and pulling me to my feet. "I'm not done with you."

From the corner of my eye, Wes begins to stir awake. He crawls onto his knees, stands up, and dives toward Gil's legs. After pinning him down, Wes looks at me and toward his pistol, but I can't move. I'm torn. Weston isn't two people merged into one, both good and bad. He's a monster. A goddamn monster. A murderer. I have moments where I want Gil to win, but he's gurgling beneath Wes.

Gil's body reacts out of desperation and rolls Wes onto

his back, allowing him to straddle his waist and wrap his hands around Weston's throat. Gil makes inhuman, guttural sounds as he strangles Wes. Blood pours from his mouth onto Weston's shirt beneath him. Weston wraps his hands around Gil's wrists and tries to pull him off, but he can't get a grip because of all the blood.

"Hannah!" he gurgles. Blood slips from the side of his mouth and drips down his cheek.

Gil's eyes are so locked on Wes, he doesn't see me grab the pistol off the ground, cock it, and fire in his direction. The bullet sears through his eye socket, and he makes a grunting sound before collapsing onto the ground beside Wes. His body twitches.

I step back and slide my body down the wall, wrapping my arms around myself despite the pain. Wes pants and spits blood, looking at me as if he were a wild animal. He can't regain his footing at first, so he crawls to me and tries to pull me into him.

"Hannah," he whispers.

I keep my eyes locked on Gil's body, finally still and lifeless. Blood pools beneath him. My mouth hangs open and my chest heaves as I cry. "I can't . . . I can't . . . I killed him!" Tears slip down my cheeks, clearing a path within the blood.

"Look at me!" Wes demands. When I don't look at him, he grabs my chin with a bloody hand and forces me to face him.

"What?" I scream at him, my voice shaking and uneven.

"You saved my life."

"I saved my own fucking life," I snap at him.

Wes tries to wrap his arms around me, but I shrink away from him.

"I don't even understand what the hell just happened!" I cry.

"You got close enough to make your shot." He shrugs and collapses onto the ground.

He chuckles at this most inappropriate time, but I, too, have laughed after a near death experience. It's a "fuck you" to the universe. Is that all you got?

CHAPTER NINETEEN

I shiver on the bed. A blood-tinged bucket of water sits next to me, along with a pink-stained white rag. I wipe the last bit of blood from my face before I put the bucket on the floor and lie down, facing the window. Wes grabs the bucket and slides it across the floor, the water sloshing as he cleans the blood off himself. He sits down beside me and reaches out to touch my arm. I flinch.

"Hannah, please talk to me."

"Is it true?" I ask without looking at him, my gaze planted on the landscape outside the window.

He wrings out the rag over the bucket, water splashing into it. "Is what true?"

"You killed all those people?" My voice is unwavering as I try to elicit the truth from him. The real truth.

He's silent for what feels like an eternity before he puts both hands in his lap and takes a deep breath. "Yes, it's true."

"You're a murderer," I say in a daze.

"You knew that already," he says with a soft smile.

Fair. I did know that. I've known it all along. Wes values

no life above his and his own. He considers me his own, and he's defended me ruthlessly. I can appreciate the sentiment, but not the reality of it. He bathes my hands in blood from acts of revenge I never asked for.

"Can we really keep this going between us?" I ask. "We aren't even on the same planet. I don't live in a world where you can just kill other people."

"If you can look past all I've done, I can show you I ain't that man now . . . mostly. I've killed, and I'll kill again if it means protecting you, but I have no interest in a lawless life any longer. I'm trying to move forward, and I want to do that with you."

His words soothe me. How can I judge him for his past when I haven't been a good person either? I played a part men wanted me to play, but in doing so, I lost the value of being myself. I've ripped marriages apart. Most importantly, I killed myself. Every day, I watched the slow bleed as life left my eyes.

You don't have to have killed to be a killer.

"Can you please look at me?" He reaches over and touches my shoulder, but I recoil from him. "Please?"

I turn over to face him, and the pain sears through my ribs, almost leaving me breathless. I look at his swollen and bruised face. A momentary pang of sympathy springs forward, but it quickly dissipates. If I had the strength, I would ride to town and get the fuck out of here.

"I can't make up for what I did, Hannah. There's just no way. I'll rot in hell for the rest of eternity. I know this already. But I want to live this life, in this heaven with you, for as long as I can."

"Well, I don't want to stay here with you." I scoff and wince from the pain.

"Please, give me a couple of days. Just a couple of days."

I can't go anywhere right now, anyway. I'll just live with this fucking serial killer.

He leaves me to fall asleep alone in the bed, but I can't get comfortable. My bones ache, and the bruises throb. He rustles through one of his drawers and pulls out a bottle of morphine, takes a swig, and hands it to me. I take it reluctantly.

"Sure you aren't going to kill me?" I roll my eyes and turn away from him. The morphine makes me groggy, my eyelids become heavy, and I welcome sleep.

HE MUST HAVE STAYED UP ALL NIGHT BECAUSE I'M up before the sun, and he's already made coffee. He brings me a mug, and I take a sip. It's much better than mine; I'll give him that. Wes sits beside me with a foot of stagnant air between us. He inches closer, but I'm too drained to fight him on it any longer. His hand reaches out and covers mine, and his other hand touches the cut on my face. His fingertips trace down my neck and over the gash in my throat.

"This place sucks," I whine as I assess my wounds.

"Here?" he asks with a pained look in his eyes.

"All of this. The nineteenth century in general." I drop back on the bed with a huff.

"Huh?"

"I'm not from this damn time. I belong in the future."

"The future? What do you mean?" He looks at me as I expected him to—like I'm crazy.

There's no way to explain any of this to Wes. I don't even think Belle believed me, though she acted like she did. We're really good actors in this line of work.

"Forget it," I say.

He looks at me curiously before wrapping me up in his arms, but I'm too tense to hug him back.

"I'll be back," he says. He leaves the house, and the door slams behind him.

I look out the window and see him carrying a shovel toward the barn. *Oh my god, is this real life right now?*

When he eventually comes back inside, his clothing is covered in sand and dust. Sweat drips down his forehead, and he nearly collapses in the chair.

"Did you just bury a fucking body on your property?" I stare at him with a slack jaw.

"What else would you like me to do? Alert the sheriff?"

His sarcastic tone pisses me off.

"Why not?" I ask.

"Oh, sheriff, my old friend who was in a gang with me came back and assaulted us over stolen jewelry we took in a robbery, and my lady friend here had to shoot him dead. Sound about right?" He smirks as he tells his elaborate story.

I roll my eyes. "Fine! I get it." I stare at him while he puts the shovel against the house. "Did you actually fuck his wife?"

"No. She was wretched." He smiles as he wipes his hands on his pants. "I would have said just about anything to get him off you." Wes touches my face. "You look better today."

"I don't feel better. Can we go into town and get more morphine?" I ask, my body craving pain relief. And opiates.

Weston touches the bruises on his face and nods. We walk outside and pull Concetta and Hickock from the pen. While Wes tacks up Hickock, I put the blanket on Concetta before hoisting the heavy saddle onto her back. I follow Weston's directions and tie the girth tightly before slipping the bridle over her head. We mount at nearly the same time.

We keep the horses at a leisurely pace because the rise

and fall of their hips causes pain that makes us flinch. I steal a glance at him. Even in his current state, I find him attractive. Every cut and bruise tugs at my heart. I could stay angry with him forever, but I don't want to. I want his arms around me and his hot breath on my neck. I want his comfort and strength. But I can't say those things; it's not my way.

My voice interrupts the stale desert air. "You know, I don't hate you for what you've done. I'm just mad you couldn't tell me the truth. I had to hear it from fucking Gil."

"I'm sorry. I was scared if you knew who I really was, you'd leave."

"That's my decision to make, not yours. Starting now, I want you to be honest with me."

He looks over with hope in his eyes. "Does that mean you'll stay?"

I hold his gaze, unable to break away. "Yes. But no more lies."

Pot, meet kettle.

A grin breaks across his face. He flinches from the pain, but he can't stop smiling. I fight back a smile of my own as we ride closer to town.

"I know it's not New York," he says, "but I'll give you the best life I can out here. We'll have—"

I gasp as The Bawdy comes into view. It's blackened and burned. The walls are charred, and the windows are covered over with planks of wood.

"Wes!" My heart sinks and melts into my stomach. *My way home!* My body fidgets, and I feel the need to get off the horse and run inside. "We have to go in there!"

"What, why?" He draws up on the reins, trying to slow Hickock to a stop.

"I just have to!"

I dismount and run toward the door of the saloon, struggling to pry it open. Pieces of the ceiling have crumbled onto the floor and tables. Most everything is destroyed, and a thick layer of soot covers what isn't.

I feel a hand on my shoulder, and I jump out of my skin, the eerie silence rubbing my nerves raw.

"I don't think we should be in here," Wes says. "It's not safe."

"I have to see."

I look over at the card table where I first met Wes. It's broken in half, and one side has disintegrated into a pile of ashes. The glasses hanging over the bar are still intact.

I walk toward the stairs. Some steps have burned through, making them impassable. I test my weight on each step, listening to the creak of straining wood under my weight. Wes follows in my footsteps. I touch the railing, and my fingertips come away black with soot.

At the top of the stairs, most of the doors are blackened or burned completely. The paintings on the walls are in various stages of decay. The fire left portions of them vividly untouched. My feet crunch along the charred carpet as I continue toward my old room. A wooden beam falls inches in front of me, and I leap backward. The walls vibrate from the force.

"Hannah, this is what I mean!"

He reaches out to grab my shoulder, but I shrug out of his grasp. I continue toward my room by climbing over the beam. Creaking wood echoes around us with an eerie cry.

I stand in front of my door. It's streaked with soot, but mostly untouched. It's the only one. I look behind me at Belle's room, and it's just a charred hole. Its depths have been ripped out and broken—much like Belle herself. I reach out my hand and grip the doorknob to my room, my heart hammering against my chest.

Despite the shaking of my hand, I manage to turn the knob. Bright sunlight shines through the doorway, forcing me to shield my eyes. Once my vision adjusts, I stand in stunned disbelief. The parking lot and my car wait just past the threshold.

I gasp and nearly fall back against Wes.

"What is that?" Wes peers around me, looking in front of us.

"You can see it too?" I gasp, my lip trembling.

Weston nods at me with his mouth agape. "What is this?"

"It's where I came from."

I turn to look at him. His eyes are wide with confusion. His warm, ragged breath falls over the back of my neck.

"I can't stay here," I say. "I have to go back."

"I don't know what's through that door," he says, "but I can't stay here without you."

I think about how overwhelming everything would be for him. I'd seen movies that somewhat prepared me for his century, so I wasn't completely shell-shocked, but every little thing would be new and scary for him. I can't bring him with me. I can't.

"You can't come."

"I want to come! I want to go where you are, wherever *that* is." He casts a suspicious glance through the door before touching my cheek.

"It's the future."

"The future?" His face twists in shock and surprise.

"I'm one hundred and thirty years past your time," I tell him.

"How did you end up here?" he asks without taking his eyes off the portal.

"This room. But I couldn't get back until now. The fire must have done something to open this up."

Wes stares at me with a blank expression on his face.

I grab his hands and wrap his arms around me. "You can't come. I need you to stay here."

He shakes his head and grabs my waist, pulling us both through the doorway. The door slams behind us.

CHAPTER TWENTY

"What are you wearing?"

I look down and see that I'm back in my skimpy dress, and I try to pull it down to cover more skin. "What are *you* wearing?" I laugh as he stands before me in a white t-shirt, jeans, and sneakers.

He touches his head. "My hat . . ."

"We'll have to get you another one," I tell him with a grin on my face.

He sucks at his teeth, annoyed. "You can't just *get* another one, Hannah."

"You sure can. Trust me."

"What is that?" He points toward my car as we walk on the paved sidewalk. His steps are awkward and slow.

"That's my horse." I gesture toward the mundane sedan in the parking lot.

"That ain't no horse, Hannah."

I open the passenger side, and he eases into the seat. I sit in the driver's seat and put the key into the ignition. The engine roars to life. I look over at Wes, and he looks back at me like a startled cat. He covers his ears and clamps his eyes shut when the music blares through the speakers. I turn it off, and he lowers his hands.

"What was that awful noise?"

"Pop music."

"Nope, don't like that." His fingers graze the leather of my seats, and he shakes his head. "This is terrible leather. What kind of low-quality cow did they use?"

"It's not cow. It's fake."

His eyes dart, following the scenery as I back out of the parking lot. *"Hannah!"* he nearly screams, and I swerve slightly.

"What?" I take a quick breath as I straighten the wheel.

"The seat is getting hot! I mean, really hot!"

I roll my eyes, reach over, and click off the heated seats. He soon relaxes.

"What is that?" He motions to the black asphalt.

"Paved roads." I answer his question patiently.

"What are those?" He points at the line of black boxes attached to wooden poles.

"Mailboxes." My voice is monotone.

"What are those buildings?"

"Stores," I snap, getting a bit annoyed with his twenty questions.

"Can we stop and get morphine?"

I roll my eyes again. "We can't just *get* morphine here. I have Tylenol at home."

"Home?" His eyes light up. His head moves along with the scenery as it flies by the window.

"I live in an apartment."

"Oh," he says, as if he knows what that means. His trust in me is apparent.

We drive in silence for a while as Wes nearly pokes his head out the car window like a dog.

"Where are the horses? The cows?" The corners of his

lips draw downward as he stares at all the buildings and homes.

"There's only a couple farms near where I live."

He cocks his head. "Where do you get your meat?"

"They deliver it to the stores."

"Oh," he says with stifled curiosity, finally allowing himself to sit back and enjoy the ride.

When we reach my apartment, I grab mail from the overflowing box. The most recent envelope is dated August 30. It felt so much longer than three weeks.

I flip on the light in my apartment and take a step inside. Cool, stagnant air hits my face and reminds me where I am. Wes stares at me blankly before following me in. I turn to put my purse and jacket away, and the lights flicker on and off. I look back to see Wes flipping the switch repeatedly.

"You don't need candles? Lamps?"

I shake my head. "We have electricity here."

"Electricity." He whispers the word, and a full body shiver causes goosebumps to form on his arms. "It's so cold in here."

"That's air conditioning. Probably the best invention in modern times."

"Modern times? What year is it?"

"It's 2021."

"It's . . . 2021?" He takes a deep breath before sitting on the couch and dropping his head in his hands.

I sit next to him and put my hand on his knee. "Wes, maybe I can take you back."

The words grab his attention, and he turns his head to face me. "Will you come back too?"

"I can't."

"Then I don't want to go back," he says.

I nod and grab his hand.

He looks around the room. "What's that?" he asks, pointing to the flatscreen on the wall.

"It's a TV." I turn it on with the remote, and it's tuned to a news station. A journalist reports as a big red banner crosses the bottom of the screen. There's video of protests and cities in disarray.

He stares in disbelief. "The pictures move?" The images reflect off his irises.

"Yep."

Wes stares at me and twirls his mustache between his fingers. "Hannah? Where's the chamber pot?"

"We have toilets here." I help him up and guide him toward my bathroom. I flick on the light and gesture toward the toilet.

His eyes are drawn to it. "There's water in it."

"Yes. You . . . you know . . . right into the water. And when you're done, you push this handle down like this." I depress the lever, and the water circles the bowl before disappearing down the drain.

"Hannah!" His eyes are as wide as saucers.

"I know." I close the bathroom door and wait just outside.

"What the hell?" he says through gritted teeth from within the bathroom, and I run inside. He managed to undo the button on his pants, but his zipper is still in place.

"I promise, I'm not getting handsy." I reach out and guide his hand to lower his zipper. As the jeans splay open, I can see the tan skin of his pelvis. I go back into the hallway, close the door, and hear his stream hitting the water. I breathe a sigh of relief as he flushes the toilet. The door swings open, and I point toward the sink. "Hey, wash your hands, mister!"

He walks over to the sink and bends down to get a closer look. His hands graze the metal handles.

"Turn it." I tell him, motioning with my hands.

He tries to push the cold-water handle toward the wall, but it doesn't budge.

"Toward you."

He pulls it toward himself, and water flows from the faucet. "Hannah, look at this!"

"I know, Wes. Use the soap. Push down on the pump."

He pushes the pump, and soap squirts into the sink. He puts his hand under it and tries again, hesitating under the water and letting it run over his skin. When he finishes washing his hands, he dries them on the front of his jeans.

"Next time, use that." I gesture toward the towel on the hook beside him, and he nods with apprehension. I go into the bathroom after him and pee inside for the first time in weeks. When I open the door, he's staring at me with curiosity. "Do you want to see what I missed the most about the future?" I ask.

He nods and follows me back into the bathroom. I turn on the shower and water flows from above. The stream is strong, and ricochets off the porcelain beneath it. Steam begins to fill the room as I pull Wes in and close the door.

I strip off his shirt and drop it onto the tile floor. He reaches his hand down to undo the button on his pants, and I notice he never zipped them up when he finished using the bathroom. The jeans fall to the floor, but he hesitates for a moment before stepping out of them. I stare at his naked body as I drop the fabric of my dress. He reaches out his hand to trace the bruises on my stomach.

"It's okay. It doesn't even hurt anymore." I glance at myself in the mirror and see the pinkish-purple bruises on my face. The ones on my torso wrap around and down my right side. It contrasts almost artistically with my pale skin. I touch my oily hair. It falls past my shoulders in messy waves. I look at myself and hardly recognize that I am me.

I step into the shower and let the hot water run down my back before motioning to Wes.

He takes a tentative step into the water and recoils. "It's hot!"

"It's not hot, it's fine. Come on." I roll my eyes as I look around at my shampoo bottles. Excitement builds at the thought of washing my hair—*really* washing it.

He steps in, and the water sprays down his chest and belly. Dirt-tinged water swirls around the drain beneath us. He groans as he wraps me in his arms under the cascade of warmth. He closes his eyes, and the water drips off his nose and hovers on his lips. Once he exhales, the droplets dissipate.

"Oh, Hannah."

"I know."

I grab the bar of soap and wash his arms, chest, and back. He drops his head back and lets the water flow through his hair. I hand him the bar of soap, and he mimics what I did for him. The heat of the water and the gentle movement as Wes runs the bar of soap along my back electrifies my skin. I reach out my hand to turn off the water, but he stops me.

He wraps his other hand around the back of my neck and pulls my face to his, pushing me against the wall and kissing me with brewing hunger. He's hard, and it's pressed against my belly as his tongue explores my mouth. The water flows over my breasts as his hands reach out to caress them. He lifts my leg and strokes himself against my inner thigh before pushing inside me. Our moans break the silence between us.

His thrusts are shallow. I wrap my arms around his neck and dig my nails into his shoulders. He pulls out and spins me around so that my hands are pressed against the warm wall of the shower. He grabs my hips and pushes inside me again. I gasp at his depth. His rhythmic thrusts push me forward, and our moans are lost in the sounds of the water.

He groans against my shoulder as his movements become slow and uneven.

He moves my hair to the other side of my neck and nuzzles into me. "I'm sorry."

"Don't apologize." I can't blame him for coming too quickly. I can't imagine how exciting that must have been and how incredible it must have felt, with all his nerve endings on fire from the warmth of the shower.

I turn off the water, step out of the shower, and wrap a towel around me. Once he joins me, I wrap one around him and tuck it into itself around his waist. Beads of water drip from his firm upper body, over his chest, and down his stomach, dissolving into the towel at his waist.

We walk out of the bathroom and shiver from the cold air in the hallway. I open my bedroom door, and the familiar scent of perfume and incense greets me.

Wes turns the light on and looks around before sitting down on the bed and bouncing. "This bed is so . . ."

"Fluffy? It's memory foam," I say as a smile creeps across my face.

He smiles and lies down, his towel spreading open and exposing him fully. I hesitate for a few moments before sitting on the bed beside him. Looking around the room, I realize I have nothing for him to wear.

"I think my old roommate left some clothes here. I'll be right back." I leave him in my room to go dig through the dresser in the spare bedroom. I find a pair of gray sweatpants, a pack of brand-new boxers, and another t-shirt. I walk back into my room and lay them out on the bed. "These should fit. I think you guys were about the same size."

He picks up the bag of boxers, opens it, and holds a pair in front of him. "What are these?"

"Boxers. You wear them under your pants."

"That seems excessive," he says as he pulls at the stretchy fabric with both hands.

"You'll thank me later. Those zippers can be very unforgiving."

He stands, pulls on the boxers, and moves his hips in them. "They seem kind of constricting. How do you go to the bathroom?"

"There's a flap in the front. You just put it through there."

He laughs and sits back down on the bed. I grab shorts and a cami and slip them on before taking a cleansing breath. I can't explain how incredible it feels to wear my own clothes.

CHAPTER TWENTY-ONE

The next morning, I wake up alone in bed. The sun shines through the window above me. "Wes?" I stand up and walk down the hallway.

He calls back to me from the kitchen. He's standing in front of the refrigerator, wearing only his boxers and letting ice fall to the floor. He releases the button once he sees me.

"What the heck is this?"

"Ice, Wes. Jesus." I rush over, pick up the ice cubes, and toss them into the sink before they melt on the tile floors.

"What's ice?"

"Frozen water. You put it in drinks to make them colder." I open the refrigerator and hand him a carton of milk after I check the date. *It's only a week past its expiration date. We ingested worse in 1885.*

I fill two glasses, and Wes grabs one, taking a hurried drink of it. His face contorts and he swallows.

"That isn't milk!" he says with a curl of his lip.

"It's processed."

"Well, it's terrible."

I rub my eyes while trying to calm myself. I wasn't this

much of a child about everything when I went to his time period. It's unequivocally better here than there. The milk isn't as good, the leather isn't the same quality, your pants have zippers . . . so what?

"I'm frustrating you," Wes says with a tight-lipped smile.

"No, I'm not frustrated with you. I just knew this would be too much for you. That's why I wanted you to stay back. Not because I wanted to leave you."

"It's not too much for me. I really am enjoying myself. I think it's strange that you can't buy morphine, that you guys use fake leather, and that your milk tastes like soap, but other than that, it's fine." He laughs and puts his hand over mine.

My phone chimes, and his eyebrows raise in question. I unlock my phone and scroll to an email from an old client. He wants to see me tonight.

"Last thing I'll ask about this morning," he says, looking over my shoulder. "What's that?"

"It's a phone. I'm responding to an email. Basically, a person living across the city can send me a message—kind of like a letter—and it comes to my phone so I can read it and respond to it. You can also access the internet on it, which is this vast network where you can find the answer to pretty much anything. Go ahead. Ask me something I wouldn't know."

"What do we make soap out of back home?"

My fingers fly across the keys, and I read the results. "Lye and animal fat, mostly."

He cocks his head as he stares down at the rectangular device. "Well. That is impressive!"

I type back to my client and tell him I'm unavailable. It physically hurts me to give up that money, but I can't leave Wes alone while I go meet a client, even for a short time. *Do I even want to meet one?* There's still an aching between my legs from my time in the shower with Wes. His fingers left a memory on my body that makes the thought of other hands seem unbearable.

"I'm hungry. What do you eat here?" he asks as he stands and rubs his belly.

I shrug my shoulders. "Want to order a pizza or something?"

"I don't know what that means, but sure," he says with a flat tone, still looking around the kitchen with wide eyes.

I pick up my phone and order a large pepperoni pizza.

Wes looks at me with his eyebrows raised. "That's it?"

"Yep. Now we wait."

I toss him his t-shirt, and he slips it over his head. We sit on the couch, and he inches toward me, so I lay my head on his chest. He puts his hand over mine as I turn on the TV and flip through the channels.

"Wait, go back!" he shouts.

I backtrack through the channels.

"There!" he says once I reach an old western TV show. He sits back against the couch, kicking his feet onto the table. His eyes are wide, and his pupils dilate as he stares at the images on the screen. "It looks like where we came from!"

"They're called westerns. It's a pretty popular genre. There's shows, movies, and even porno about it."

"Shows? Movies? Porno?" His attention snaps to me, his jaw slack.

"Shows are a series of events that follow a plot in every episode. Movies are a longer 'show' but with one plot for the whole two hours." I immediately regret mentioning porn. "Well, porn is where two or more people have sex on film. It's a moving picture like this."

"They film that?" Wes curls his lip at the thought. He came from a place where missionary sex with your housewife was all the rage.

"Oh, yes. It's a whole industry here."

He sits quietly for a moment. "Can I see the porno?"

I roll my eyes and grab the laptop, pulling up my favorite website—bookmarked and all. I click a random video on the first page, and it starts to play. Wes stares as a woman in short shorts stands on the side of the road with a broken-down bicycle. An attractive man pulls up and offers to bring her back to his place to fix the bike, and she goes with him because stranger danger isn't a thing in these videos.

Wes doesn't pay any mind to the scantily clad woman on the screen, focusing only on the bike. "What is that?"

"A bicycle. It lets you drive around if you don't have a car. It's better than walking."

"No one rides horses at all?" he says with disappointment.

"You can't really do that on the roads." I fast forward a bit, and when I hit play, the room is filled with moans and groans.

Weston's eyes widen before he reaches for the lid of the laptop and closes it. "That's enough of that."

He turns his attention back to the TV, where two men in cowboy hats square off for a duel in the middle of town. They draw their pistols and shoot to kill. Wes sits up. "That's not how things happened."

"I mean, it kind of did with you and the bandits."

"Well, yes, I guess, but you don't have a shootout in the middle of town. You don't shoot people in town."

"Wes?" I cock my head at him, reminding him—with my expression—of Beak's body right outside the Bawdy. In the middle of town.

"Well, that was different. This shootout is happening because of poker. When we lose like that, we go home and lick our wounds and try to win it back next time."

I laugh, and he pulls me closer to him.

The doorbell rings, and I answer the door. The delivery

man hands me the pizza, and I reach down and grab a box that was left outside. I put the box on the table and bring the pizza over to Wes. The room fills with the heavenly aroma of spices and melted cheese as I open the lid, grab a slice, and take a bite.

Wes does the same and groans softly. "This is good! What did you call it again? Pita?"

"Pizza . . . za."

He smiles and takes another bite. "What was in the other box?" he asks with a full mouth.

"Oh! I ordered it for you yesterday."

He cocks his head at me.

"I used my phone to put in an order, and they delivered it to my house."

"Like the pizza." He nods as he blows on another slice before putting it into his mouth. Sauce drips down his chin, and he wipes it away with the back of his hand.

"I guess I didn't think of it that way, but yeah, kind of like the pizza."

I cut open the box on the table and pull out a leather cowboy hat. I walk over to Wes and hand it to him. He wipes his greasy hands on his jeans instead of the napkins before picking up the hat. His eyes close as he rubs his fingers along the grain of the leather.

"This is good leather! Good quality cowhide." He puts the hat up to his nose and sniffs deeply, as if reminiscing about his home. He places it over his thick, wavy hair and tips it toward me. "That'll do." He opens the pizza box and takes another slice. "What else can you order?"

"Pretty much anything."

He nods and starts watching the movie again. A scene plays of a man having loud sex with a prostitute, and Wes doesn't look away as he leans over to put the crust on the table. "It's porno!"

I laugh and wipe my mouth with a napkin before picking up the discarded crusts and throwing them in the garbage. When I sit back down beside him, I draw my legs up under me.

Weston turns toward me and gestures toward the TV with his chin. "They just mentioned that blowjob thing you told me about before. They don't do those back home—not even in the bordellos."

"How many times have you gone to brothels?" I ask, lifting an eyebrow.

Wes shrugs. "A few times."

"Wes!" I smack his arm playfully.

"It gets mighty lonely sometimes," he says with a heavy drawl to his words.

I blow my hair from my forehead. "You didn't even try to pay for me."

Wes stares at me, as if trying to figure out what to say. "I heard around town that you were cold. As a wet blanket, if you want to be specific." He notes the agitation on my face and tries to backpedal. "But clearly, you aren't!"

"Right. If I was so 'cold,' why did you pay to not sleep with me?"

"Well, it started off as curiosity, but then you ended up being as addictive as that morphine."

"Curiosity?" I am not a fucking side show. I don't understand what led Wes and Holden to feel such curiosity toward me.

"I've never met a woman from a whore house so willing to give the mitten."

"Give the mitten? What the hell does that mean?" I ask.

"Reject someone."

I think for a moment and realize I'm being a little harsh. I forget how much different that time period was for women—that I was different from the others there. Unique doesn't always mean better, though. I wasn't a good whore there, unlike how I'd been here.

"What can I say? I'm picky."

"I am too," he whispers. He leans in and kisses me softly, looking up at me with his brown eyes.

His kiss ignites me, and I straddle his lap. I let his tongue explore my mouth. He groans against my lips as his hands graze unfamiliar fabric, and his fingers come to rest at my hips.

"As much as I'd like to just stay in and romp in the sheets all day, I think we should get out of the house," I say.

He lets out a loud groan of frustration. "I can't get enough of you, Hannah."

"Well, there'll be plenty of time for that."

He nods and looks out the window beside him. "Didn't you say there's a farm nearby?"

"There's a cattle ranch about five miles south of here."

"Will they let us visit?" Excitement oozes from his pores at the thought of being around a farm again.

I shrug my shoulders. "There's only one way to find out."

I stand up and walk toward my room to get dressed. I slip off my nighttime shorts and pull on a pair of denim shorts. They're slightly loose on my thighs. If there's one other good thing about 1885, it's that I left about fifteen pounds back there. I slip on a new cami, and my bra straps peek out from under its thin strings.

Weston knocks and walks into my room. "Why did you change into undergarments?"

"They aren't undergarments." I tug at the fabric of my shorts.

He reaches over and touches the thin straps of my cami and purses his lips. "They're undergarments."

"Fine! If it makes you feel better, I'll wear another shirt."

"It does."

I'm not the type to let a man determine what I wear, but Wes has enough to adapt to without an argument about attire.

I reach into my closet and grab a light plaid shirt. Wes nods in approval and strips his boxers off before slipping on a new pair and pulling on a pair of jeans. He grips the pull tab, zipping and unzipping them repeatedly.

"Buttons worked just fine," he says. "I don't know why they had to add this contraption. Why fix something that ain't broken?"

"You'll find that a lot here."

CHAPTER TWENTY-TWO

M y car comes to a stop just in front of the steer-shaped sign for the Olsens' farm. We get out and shield our eyes from the kicked-up dust.

A woman in a plaid shirt comes out and greets us. "Are you here for the rodeo? There's only the cutting competition left. Sign-ups are by the arena if you're interested."

We nod and walk toward the arena. Weston's wide eyes take in the scenery around him. There's a large wooden paddock with a herd of young cattle hovering close together in the center, and Wes breathes deeply.

"Now, that's the smell of home." He looks over at the horses hitched by the arena. "You guys ride the same here?"

"Yes, that hasn't changed much. One of the few things that hasn't."

There's a sign-up sheet on a long table with a blonde teenager sitting behind it, and Wes beelines for it.

"Wes, don't do what you're thinking. This isn't how you stay under the radar!" I yell toward him, but he waves me off. When I walk up to the table, he's already talking with the young girl.

"You keep the white cow cut from the rest of the herd. Do you want to sign up? Most of the good ones have already been taken, but you can use any of the leftover horses over there."

He nods his head up and down, and she hands him a pen, which he stares at for much too long. The young girl grows impatient and hands him a pen with the nib already exposed. After eyeing the paper, he creates a scribble next to the spot marked Name. He walks over to the horses, and I grab the pen and write "Wes" next to his scribble.

"Sorry about that," I tell her with a quick smile.

I follow after Wes and find him touching various parts of the horses. He rubs his hand down their legs and lifts their hooves. He rubs the neck of a jet-black horse and leans his head into her.

Mrs. Olsen comes over and tells him he's up next after the break, which makes me sweat—not because of the heat, but because I don't want Wes to be embarrassed. I don't want to draw unnecessary attention to him, either. He rubs his hand down the leather saddle, grabs the horn, and mounts. He looks so comfortable on horseback, and I realize now why this was so important to him.

"I don't have spurs or boots," he says.

"Work with what you got."

He nods and urges his horse toward the gate and into the arena. His eyes lock on a small white calf in the center of the herd.

"Last up is a new entry," says the announcer. "It's Wes on top of At Hellion's Gate. Again, we thank you for coming to our annual 'please help keep us out of bankruptcy' ranch competition. Yeehaw!"

At Hellion's Gate? This is not *going to go well.* I sit down to watch the event and become obscure within the wall of plaid.

Hellion lifts her head and snorts. The bell tolls, and Wes

guides his horse through the herd as they separate around him. He locks on to the white calf, and it bellows as Wes separates it from the group. Wes and the horse work in sync, as if they are extensions of each other. Hellion's legs pound the sand as she follows the movement of the calf trying so tenaciously to join up with his herd. The calf tries to bolt left, and Wes blocks his path. The calf dodges to the right, but Wes is on him.

He urges the calf in a larger arc away from the others, widening the distance he must work from. The calf slips through the opening, but Wes urges Hellion between them. She works obediently, and Wes never loses his seat, feeling every movement before she makes it. The bell tolls again, and Wes takes off his hat, gesturing toward the herd as the calf retreats toward them. He walks out of the arena and dismounts with a smile on his face.

I run up to him and wrap my arms around him. "You did amazing!" I notice the flirty stares from some of the women in the crowd, so I kiss him—almost possessively.

"That was something else!" He takes off his hat and kisses me back.

Mrs. Olsen clears her throat behind us, and we both turn around. "Wes, is it?"

"Yes, that's me, ma'am."

"Impressive moves out there. Where did you learn to ride like that?"

Wes and I look at each other with a smirk.

"I grew up around horses and cattle." His eyes light up.

"Ah, well, I was wondering if you might want a job here. We need another ranch hand, and you definitely have the skills we're looking for."

Wes looks at me for guidance. How will he explain away his curiosity over normal, modern things? I don't know if this is the best thing for him to do, but where else can he get a job without a background, bank account, or even an identity. He's handled everything so far with couth and an open mind, so I nod.

"I'll take the job. It would be an honor."

She looks down at his sneakers. "You would have to get yourself a pair of boots, though."

After they work out the details, we walk toward my car. Wes struts the whole way.

"Did you see that, Hannah? That horse was incredible! She moved just like Concetta. There's something about those big charcoal mares, I swear. They're drawn to cattle like flies to shit."

"You're so poetic, but yes, I did see it, and it was pretty incredible."

"I felt so alive. As if both our worlds merged in that moment." His eyes drop, his lips drawing down. "Concetta . . ." he whispers. "What do you reckon happened to my horses?"

"I don't even know what happened with us—what kind of time warp we were in. Is everything just gone as if it never existed? Does life carry on without us? Seems this side of time carried on without me. Without going back, I'm not sure we'll ever know."

The disappointment is clear on his face as we climb into the car. He stares out the window at the black mare tied up outside the arena. She's covered in white froth. "She's so familiar."

"Who?"

"That dang horse. It's like we knew each other. For a little while, I forgot I left Concetta behind."

"When are they announcing the winners?" I ask, trying to change the subject.

"I don't know. They said they'd post the results in the book of faces."

I laugh. "I'll follow them and let you know."

He looks down at his mud-covered sneakers. "We need to go get boots."

I nod, and we drive toward the city. I pull into a large parking lot and park in front of an outdoor sports store. We step out of the car and head toward the automatic doors, which open and make Wes jump backward.

"Hannah!"

"It's just an automatic door. It uses electricity to open when it senses a person." I walk into the store and turn to see Wes stepping in and out of the view of the sensor so the door would open and close.

He laughs and catches up with me.

"I wish I enjoyed things half as much as you do," I say as he looks around the store with wide eyes. It's the way a child looks in a toy store, filled with excitement and wonder.

We walk through the camping aisle, and Weston stops to look at me after eyeing the display tents.

"They're tents. It's for when you go camping."

"Camping?" Wes cocks his head.

"You go out into the wilderness and pitch a tent to sleep in."

He rubs his hand against the taut fabric of the tent. "People leave all those nice things they have at home just to go sleep outside on the ground?"

I can't help but laugh at the genuine disbelief on his face. "Yes, we do." I used to like to camp to disconnect from technology, but I've had enough disconnecting to last me the rest of my life.

We head down an aisle filled with kits for model planes, ships, and cars. Wes reaches out and touches one before picking it up and examining it.

I notice his interest. "It's an airplane."

"What's it do?"

"You'll see them flying in the sky sometimes. There are lots of people inside, and it flies them from one place to another. It's how I got from New York to here."

"You were in one of these?"

"Yes, but they're much bigger than that. Probably as big as this whole store."

"Wild." He laughs softly and puts the plane back on the shelf.

"Where did you get that word from?"

"I heard it on the TV. It describes the future pretty well."

I shrug because he's not wrong.

We turn a corner and finally find the men's clothing section. Wes is drawn toward the rack of plaid shirts, grabbing one of every color and pushing them into my hands before flying to another rack. He grabs a couple more jeans and hands them to me. None are the correct size, so I put them back and grab his size in everything he handed me as he goes to look in the next aisle.

I walk around the corner and find him trying on different boots. Boxes and shoes are strewn about the walkway. An employee walks by to greet us. She sees the mess, gives us a look, and walks past us, shaking her head.

"You can't just make a mess here," I tell him as I try to pick up some of the boxes.

"Sorry, but look at these. They're perfect!" He stands up and takes a few steps in a pair of brown cowboy boots that are almost as dark as his eyes.

"Do you really think this is a good idea?"

"These boots?" he switches the weight from one leg to the other, popping his hip out. "Yes."

"No, you working at the ranch. What if you're exposed to something you don't know how to react to or use? I can't explain things to you if I'm not there."

"Come work there too?"

A look of disbelief crosses my face.

"Why not?" He purses his lips.

"I'm not spending my days cleaning up shit. Absolutely not." I take a deep breath because I know I only have two options. I can either get a different job, or I need to get back to my clients.

CHAPTER TWENTY-THREE

"Fucking Wes," I mumble under my breath as I scoop a pile of horse manure with the spiked shovel.

He pops up from the stall next to mine and flings shit into the bucket. "What did you say?"

"Nothing. I was just talking to myself."

"That's a sign of being unwell, you know," he says with a smirk.

I fake a smile at him.

"I may not be all too savvy with how you guys talk yet," he says, "but I can tell when you're upset. That body language has been around long before my time."

"I'm not annoyed with you. I'm frustrated that I had to give up my *really* good paying job for this."

"I don't want you to be unhappy. If you want to go back to your other job, just do it."

"I don't think you understand what you're asking me to do."

Wes puts the end of the shovel down on the ground and rocks the handle in his hands, leaning his weight on it. "No?"

I lower my voice to a whisper. "I sleep with people for money."

He drops his shovel and wipes his hands on his pants. "You get paid a lot for that?"

"First off, rude, but yes," I say with a squint of my eyes.

"I would prefer that you didn't go back to your other job if it means you have to have sex with anyone else." He smiles at me in the way only he can—a naive grin that melts me.

"Now you see why I'm frustrated?"

He walks over and leans in to kiss me. He picks up the bucket I've filled and carries it out of the barn. From the corner of my eye, I see one of the Olsen daughters. She and Wes laugh as they come back down the aisle. She gives me a dirty look. I roll my eyes as I turn off the hose in the water bucket.

"Let me help you with that," she says as she grabs the other side of the manure bin from the stall Wes had been working on.

"Why, thank you," he says. They each grab one side and carry it back down the hallway and out the backdoor.

I finish rolling up the hose and wipe the dirt off my hands. At least I hope it's just dirt.

"Hello?" I call out. *Where the hell is he?*

Silence.

I walk toward the back of the barn and find the Olsen girl pinning Wes against the door and kissing him. His hands flail for a moment before he stops fighting her advances. I clear my throat, and she backs away, pretending to be startled. She smirks at me, wipes her mouth, and turns to walk away. Wes stares at her for a moment too long.

I raise my arm out to the side and point toward my car without looking at him. *"Now!"*

We sit in the car, and I turn on the ignition to raise the

windows. I twist my body toward him and let my hands rest intertwined on my lap.

"Hannah, what did I do?"

"I'm going to fucking remind myself that you aren't from this time, and that somehow in 1885, it was okay for you to make out with someone else." I belt out a humorless laugh.

"Well, it kind of was if you weren't married or nothing."

I take a deep breath and rub the bridge of my nose. "So, let me just make sure I understand what you're saying. You can kiss another woman, but I can't do my other job?"

"Kissing used to be akin to a handshake sometimes. I didn't think she meant nothing by it. She didn't even ask me for any money."

"Jesus, Wes! She isn't a prostitute. Unlike 1885, most of the women here aren't. She's flirting with you. She wants to sleep with you!" I throw my hands up in frustration.

"But not a prostitute?"

"No. Here, we flirt and court people for relationships. Hell, sometimes even just a one-night stand. We don't just pay each other for sex."

"But, Hannah?" He cocks his head and gestures toward me.

Touché. It's hard to argue that point. "Do you want to be with me or not? If you want to sow your wild oats, by all means, go ahead, but you won't be with me while you do it."

He looks down at his lap and reaches out his hand to cover mine. "I'm sorry. I do want to be with you. These lips will only be for you." He laughs and smacks his lips together.

"Ok," I say. I'm not sure he knows what he really wants. It was easier when there were only two dozen women in the whole town.

This is an insecurity I'm unfamiliar with. I've never given ultimatums or denied the reality of human attraction and sexuality. I would probably allow the Olsen girl to kiss me, too, if she tried. I'm a walking contradiction.

"I have to get back and work the horses," he says as he grabs my trembling hand.

I nod and roll the windows down. "I'll watch from here."

He looks back at me as if he should stay, but he's drawn to the horses. He jogs over to Hellion, mounts her, and urges her into the arena. He takes a few laps at a walk before coaxing her into a floaty trot. Using his seat, he stops her suddenly and turns her, repeating it several times in both directions.

Diana comes out and leans against the arena fence. Her breasts are perky, and she has such a petite form, which makes me jealous for a moment.

Wes dismounts and leads Hellion back toward the hitching post. He hands the reins off to Diana, who takes them and leans her chest into Wes. She laughs as she touches his arm, and I scoff because I know those moves and have used them more times than I can count. She leans in to kiss him again, and I grip the handle of the door so hard my knuckles turn white. I watch him lean away from her and put his hand out. I can't tell for sure, but he seems to be gently letting her down. He gestures in the same calm, suave way he did with the madam, and with a nod, she turns to lead Hellion toward the barn.

Wes comes back to the car and sits next to me. "Diana tried to kiss me again."

"I saw." My words are woven with annoyance.

"I told her I'm with you," he says.

I know he did, so why does it still bother me so much? When I was back in his time, I was new, different, and exciting. I could understand why there was an allure about me. Here, I'm none of those things. I guess Wes is right. I am unwell.

We drive home in silence and head into the apartment.

Wes strips off his clothes at the door and flops down on the couch in his boxers, gesturing toward them. "You were right about these things. They're great."

"I'm glad you like them," I say with a huff as I drop my bag onto the ground. The sound vibrates the pans on the counter.

"Come here," he commands.

I shake my head softly.

"Come here, Hannah!" This is the first time Wes has gotten stern with me. It takes me by surprise and draws me to him with curiosity. He touches my lips with his fingertips, trailing them down my chin and neck. "Do you think I think less of you because of the job you had? Both here and there? Is that what this is about?"

"No . . . yes . . . I don't know. No one wants to wed a whore."

Belle's words still echo in my head, long after her final breath left her lungs. They resonate with me, not just because I've always felt that way, but because she's correct. He may never fully trust me, and he might never feel my honor is high enough to be a wife—as if I'm soiled until the day I die.

He lifts my chin. "I told you not to call yourself that."

"It's what I am, Wes."

He rises and leans over me, his arms firmly planted on either side. He kisses me with a gentle passion. "If that's really the case, then I *do* want to wed a whore." He whispers the words against my mouth as he unbuttons my shirt. He grasps at my bra. "Not the time, I know, but what the hell is that?"

"It's a bra. It keeps our ladies in their assigned seats."

"Okay, now *that* seems excessive."

"It might be, but I'd wear a bra over a corset any day." I smirk up at him.

He fumbles with different areas of the bra, trying to figure out how to get it off, and I roll my eyes.

"There's clasps on the back," I say.

He leans over, examines the buckle, and reaches behind me to unclip my bra. It falls past my arms, and I let it slip onto the floor. While he takes off his hat and sets it down on the ground, I pull my shorts down my thighs. He slips his boxers off his waist and kicks them away with a devilish grin on his face.

He leans back into me for a kiss before his lips trail down my neck and focus their attention on the soft skin of my breasts. His hands take the place of his mouth, and he presses his hips into me. I groan at the heat of him against me. I can nearly feel his heartbeat through his cock. He thrusts into me, and I moan loudly as he uses my hips to meet his movement. He pauses to let me feel the full length of him inside me.

"Hannah," he whispers into the air between us before leaning over and kissing me. Our lips embrace and spread to explore one another's mouths. "Do you think any other woman could do this to me the way you do?"

His words are meant as a compliment, but they anger me. I want to scream that yes, they probably could. I don't think he realizes that my confidence is a ruse. Just because I've fucked more often, it doesn't make me any better at it than anyone else. He, on the other hand, can do such unearthly things to my body. Maybe because he is out of this world. My body complements his ability, but his talent holds its own just as easily without me.

He touches my cheek and reins me back in. I'm so used to wandering the depths of my mind in these moments, no matter how destructive it may be. His lips draw me from my thoughts and lay my vulnerability out for him to devour. He doesn't swallow me whole like other men have, ridding me of my identity. Wes takes bites out of me and replaces them with parts of himself in return. He makes me feel feelings, and I don't know if I want that responsibility.

He kisses me and wraps his arm around me so that my head is in the crook of his elbow. He brushes the hair back from my face. "I love you, Hannah."

I feel a pang in my gut that isn't from pleasure as his hand reaches around my heart and squeezes. It's a warm and loving embrace, but in my head, I am breathless and suffocating. I pull away and sit up, which surprises him.

"I care about you so much, Wes, but I don't know what to do with your love. I don't deserve this. Any of this." I fight back tears.

Wes sits speechless for a moment, looking defeated. "I wouldn't be here right now if it weren't for you. Not just here in this time, but here at all. Gil would have killed me."

I disappear into the memory of shooting Gil. I remember the blood pouring from his head and his body's final movements. I can still smell the sweet, metallic scent of the crimson liquid mixed with the noxious sulfur fumes of the smoking gun in my shaking hand. This memory will forever be woven into the fabric of my mind.

"I know, Wes."

"What if I said I wanted to marry you and have a child with you?"

My expression twists, and I can feel my lips draw sideways. "I would tell you that you don't know what you want."

"Could you be with child?"

"No, absolutely not." *I don't think.* I don't have regular cycles because of my implant, but I've silently prayed that it remained within the flesh of my arm many times. "I'm on birth control."

"Birth control?"

"It's this device with hormones that prevents pregnancy." I rub the area of my arm where the contraption is embedded. Hopefully.

"Why would you want to do that?" His lips form a frown as he looks down at me.

"Because most children survive past five years old now, and some people aren't ready for that kind of commitment."

He rests a hand on my stomach. I know he has an ache in his balls for children, having lost his child alongside his wife. I don't know that I can be what he needs me to be—a mother or a wife.

"Wes?"

"What?" He brushes hair out of my face.

"I think you should go back. I'm wasting your time. We could live to be one hundred years old here, and I may never be what you need."

His hand stills on my cheek. "I don't know how I can prove to you that you *are* what I need. I was living an empty, lonely, and unforgiving existence before I met you. I have smiled, laughed, and seen more with you than I ever thought possible. How would I not need you?"

I sit up on my elbow. "Because sometimes we don't always fall in love with the people who are best for us. Sometimes our hearts can't tell the difference."

"Well, I don't believe you're correct. I may not be from this time, but I know what love is. I don't know what made you so jaded that you can't see what's right in front of you." He stands and brushes his hands through his hair.

"Wes."

"No, you can't tell me who I am or am not in love with!" He shakes his head. He's almost yelling. Almost.

"Wes!"

"I'm pouring my heart out to you, and you just don't

care." He looks at me with such fierce intensity, it makes me recoil. His lips are taut.

I pull Wes down on the chair and put my hands on his shoulders, bracing myself. "I've been sexually abused for as long as I can remember. Sex has never meant the same for me as it does for you. I have been beaten and nearly killed more times than I can count, and sex is always the common factor. This has all happened in *my* time. You may have lived in an anarchic town, but I have lived a lawless life here of my own. I have lived a life where a man can rip me apart and walk right out the door with my very essence. Not even just one man—maybe I could have handled that."

Tears well in his eyes and his hands tremble.

"I don't think I'm capable of love because it's been stripped from my naked body. My heart has begun to beat for you, Wes, but I don't know if I like the feel of its pulse in my chest. It's made of glass, and I'm afraid it'll shatter if I continue to let myself feel."

He wraps me in his arms, and I sob against his chest. If I show weakness, I'm fragile. If I'm fragile, I'm breakable. I built an impenetrable wall around myself, and Wes has been the only person able to dig beneath it. He is within the prison of my own construction, but it's not fair for him to be trapped here.

"I'm sorry for everything that has ever happened to you," he says. "You know I would kill every man who has ever harmed you, but I can't do that here. I can only take care of you and protect you now. I can't make up for the past, but I can try to replace what others have stolen from you. Just give me the chance to do it. Let me make you whole again." He lies down on the couch and pulls me into him, wrapping his strong arms around me.

In these moments, I feel safe, as if he's my sanctuary.

Wes holds me as he rubs his hand up and down my side.

He lets me cry until I'm empty. I let the shame and hesitation leave my body as tears, and I melt into his touch.

"I don't want you to leave," I say as I turn over to look at him.

He stops rubbing my side and brushes the hair out of my face. "I wasn't going to, anyway," he says with a shrug. "I promised to take care of you, and I intend on doing just that."

Wes is everything I need, even if I don't feel like I can be what he needs. He's too stubborn to let me go, and I'm too stubborn to let myself love. I need to stop doing that. Despite being unable to let the words loose from my throat, I can still read them. I can still understand them.

Wes looks at me with his eyebrows drawn. "I know this isn't the time, but do you guys really live to a hundred years old here?"

He's the only one who can make me smile despite my tear-streaked cheeks.

"Sometimes, yes."

"Oh, well, that changes everything. I thought we'd only be together for another fifteen or twenty years at the most. Eighty more years just seems excessive." He laughs, squeezes me tightly, and kisses my shoulder.

"I'd go back with you to your time, but twenty years with you isn't quite long enough for me." I kiss him.

We're still naked, and the heat between our bodies is palpable. He hardens and rubs his hand along his cock. "Remember the blowjob you gave me?" he whispers as he stretches.

"Yeah?"

"Can I give you one?"

I laugh and nod. "We don't really call it that, but I get what you're asking." I shouldn't render my body for use so readily, but with him, it solves everything. My doubt, my fear, my insecurities—they dissolve at his touch. He'll make me come, and I'll forget the turmoil I put myself in.

"What's it called?" he asks curiously.

I smile at him, my eyelashes fluttering. "Cunnilingus, eating out, going down, or just oral sex."

"Cunn-il-lingus." He exaggerates the word.

"Oh lord, just call it going down on me."

He nods as he pushes me onto my back. Goosebumps rise on my body from the sudden change in temperature as he crawls between my legs.

"Tell me what to do."

"Kiss my thighs," I whisper, and he obliges. I shiver. "Lick me."

He reacts to my command without hesitation. His warm tongue is against me, moving up and down. The heat of his mouth caresses my skin, and his mustache tickles me in all the right ways. I reach down, take a fistful of his hair, and pull him closer. My thighs quiver as he laps at me.

"Oh, Wes," I moan into the silence of the room.

He grabs my hips as I grind against his mouth, more in the moment than I have ever been. My mind is silent, which is an unusual treat. Who knew that Wes would be the remedy for my ailing mind? The aching feeling in my gut grows, and my body tightens and tenses. I grip the fabric beneath me as I come harder than I ever have.

Wes climbs up to me and wipes his mouth before kissing me, but I can still taste myself on his tongue. He grabs my hips and pulls them up, and then he's quickly inside me. I'm hypersensitive to his deep and unforgiving thrust. My nerve endings are wide awake, and every touch and feeling is amplified.

"Hannah," he whispers against my mouth as he leans down to kiss me.

His thrusts get stronger but slower. He reaches his hand

between my legs and rubs me. Wes kisses along my collar-bone, taking his time with every spread of his lips, as if absorbing my essence. The fire ignites and heats me from the inside out, making my skin feel hot.

"Put your hand around my throat, Wes," I plead through hitched breaths.

"Hannah . . ." I can feel and hear his hesitation.

"Just do it!" I command.

With an exhale, he reaches his hand up and wraps it around my throat.

"Squeeze."

"Choke you?" he says with surprise.

"Just a little," I whisper.

He takes a deep breath and tightens his grip on my neck. I can feel the throbbing beats of my pulse against his hand. I groan as he thrusts harder. He drops his face into the crook of my neck, a low passionate groan tantalizing my skin.

"You're incredible," he whispers into my ear.

The heat between my legs rises as my legs quiver. The pleasure crashes over me like a wave as I come. It covers my body, saturates me, and leaves me trembling.

Chapter Twenty-Four

I wake up the next morning in Wes's arms. He pulls me into him as I try to get out of bed.

"Do you think we can go to my old farm?" he asks as he props up on his elbow. His expression is soft and comfortable as he stifles a yawn.

"Back to 1885?" I ask. *Why would he want to go back?*

He touches my arm and shakes his head. "No, not back then. Now."

"I doubt it's still a thing, Wes."

"Can we try?" His eyes are large and pleading—almost childlike.

I smile at him and nod. "We can go to the library and see if they have deeds," I tell him with cautious optimism. "But don't get your hopes up. It's been a long time since then." I lean down and kiss him. "Let's get dressed."

We throw on our clothes as Wes's excitement grows. As we exit the apartment, he grabs a gardening shovel leaning up against the building that's been there since yesterday. He tosses it into the trunk.

"Shovel? Am I going to be murdered?"

"No, I have something at the farm I want to dig up." He grins at me.

"Are you as hungry as I am?" I ask him as my stomach pleads for food.

"I can always eat." He looks out the window as we start to drive. He rolls it down and sticks his arm out, waving his hand in the wind.

We pull into the drive-through of a fast-food restaurant. When I drive up to the speaker, a voice booms out of the box. The crackly feedback is distracting.

"What the . . ." Wes stares at the box, and I put my finger up to signal him to hold on.

"Can I have two number threes, please?" I turn to look at Wes. "Do you want cheese on your breakfast sandwich?"

Wes shakes his head, his gaze still locked on the talking box.

I turn back to the speaker. "One with cheese, please."

When we pull up to the next window, I pay and take the bag of food. I park and hand Wes his sandwich and drink. He unwraps it and stares at it.

"It's a sausage biscuit." I smile at him as I take a bite of mine. My stomach welcomes the warm food, and I eat much too fast.

He takes a bite of his, and his eyes roll back. "Why is the food so incredible here?" He groans as he inhales his meal. He tosses the wrapper back in the bag and wipes the grease onto his pants.

We leave the restaurant and pull into the library parking lot. The building is massive, and Wes's eyes rise up the height of it as he closes the car door.

"Wow," he whispers.

We walk through the door, and the silence in the building absorbs us. Wes looks around at the walls of books and the string of computers. The woman at the front desk closes her book and stands to greet us.

"How can I help you?" she asks as she puts her glasses on top of her head.

"Do you have deeds here?" I ask, approaching the desk.

Wes stands behind me, soaking in the old building stuffed to the brim with all the knowledge one could need.

"Yes, we have county records." She walks us over to a large cabinet full of thick books. The age of the books goes from oldest to newest, their ages apparent from the conditions of the covers. "What year?" she asks.

"Pre 1885." I look over her shoulder.

"Quite some time ago." She smiles as she grabs an old blue book and places it on the table beside the cabinet.

I touch it, feeling the aged leather under my fingertips. "Thank you." I smile at her, pull out a chair, and take a seat. I thumb through the book of deeds. "They've been typed up from the original documents, it seems. They still have the coordinates, but they're sorted by fucking date." I look at Wes. "I'm guessing you don't know when the actual Weston Willebrand bought the property, huh?"

"I think it was 1875. I remember finding some paperwork at the farm."

I nod and flip the pages backward until I get toward 1875. I slide my fingers down the page as I look for the familiar name. "This is going to take forever." I sigh as I flip the next page and keep looking.

I finally find the name on the second to last page. I snap a picture of the recorded information and accidentally slam the book closed. It echoes throughout the library, and the woman at the desk shoots me a dirty look.

Let's go, I mouth to Wes as I place the book back on the shelf.

We head to the car, and I plug the coordinates into my

phone and place it in the holder on my dashboard. The robotic voice begins giving directions. Wes stares at it.

"It's GPS. I don't know how people survived without it." I smile at him.

"We survived fine. There weren't many places to go back where I came from." He shakes his head and chuckles.

We drive toward the Bawdy Way Motel but pass the exit. We take the next one and continue east. The road is older and unkept, and the homes are far from each other. Corn fields rise up on both sides of the pavement. Wes stares out the window.

"In a half mile, your destination will be on the right," the GPS announces.

I look at the map as I try to figure out where I'll be stopping. We pull in front of an older home with a for sale sign out front. It's large and white, and it looks abandoned.

"This is 4224 Riley Way, built in 1905," I say as we step out of the car.

The farm has changed from when we were here, though the landscape has remained mostly intact. I shield my eyes from the sun and look around. A haunting familiarity sends a shiver down my spine.

"This is definitely the land," I say, looking at Wes.

His eyes are locked, as if he's envisioning the structure of his old farm: the round pen with the horses, the small house, and the large barn behind it. He walks toward the back of the house and finds a newer barn where the old one had been. He smirks as he runs back to the car and grabs the shovel from the trunk.

"What are you doing?" I yell as he jogs toward the back of the barn.

I catch up to him and see him counting his steps from the back left corner of the structure, heel over toe. He forces the blade of the shovel into the ground, and a puff of dust rises up, enveloping him. I sit down along the wall of the barn, the hot metal against my back. He digs until sweat drips from his brow and down his cheeks. More collects under his arms and down his back, darkening his shirt.

"Again, what are you doing?"

"I don't know if it's here." His words are quick and clipped as he steps on the blade of the shovel, pushing it deeper into the ground. The clink of metal hitting metal sings out, and he looks at me with a smile. He lets the shovel fall to the ground, drops to his knees, and starts dusting sand off the rusted box. He pulls it out of the earth and places it on the ground in front of him. The smile grows on his face as he picks up the shovel and smashes the blade against the rusty lock, popping it open. He eases back the lid.

"What is it?" I stand and walk over to him. I lean down and look at the contents of the box. My eyes widen and my eyebrows rise at the sight of expensive jewelry. The pieces shimmer in the sun, and I dig my hand around the precious metals and jewels. "This is . . ." I gasp.

"Yes. It is." Weston stands and flashes a broad smile.

I stare at him with squinted eyes, fighting back the temptation to smack him across the face. When I take a step toward him, he takes a step back.

"What's wrong?" He puts his arms out in front of him, the sweat beading on his tanned skin.

"You almost got me killed, and you had this *all along?*" I raise my voice and step against his outstretched hands.

"I . . . I just . . ." He stumbles over his words. "What was I supposed to do?"

"I don't know, give it to him? I got beat for this! People got killed for this jewelry, Wes!" I turn away from him as my anger rises like the temperature. "How can you say you cared about me when you let that happen to me. You acted like you didn't have it!"

Wes comes up behind me and wraps his warm arms around me, squeezing me.

"I'm sorry," he whispers. The familiar smell of dirt and sweat wafts toward my nose. "I should have told you, but I felt like I had the situation with Gil handled at the time."

"*Handled?* You'd be dead if I hadn't shot him. Nothing about that situation was *handled.*"

"It was safer if you didn't know about this. Do you know how much this is worth now?" He leans down and picks up the box and shakes it. "You don't have to do that job anymore. With this, I can take care of you in ways I couldn't in my time." He puts his face against mine and takes a deep breath. "I love you," he whispers against my mouth.

Chapter Twenty-Five

W e drive the long, winding roads we've driven only once before. Wes still glances around as the sun causes glares to dance on the windshield. He never seems to get used to the modern world that I have thrust him into.

We pull into the parking lot, and Wes immediately recognizes it as the motel. "Why are we here?" His calm expression is blanketed with anxiety and fear.

"Don't panic. I just want to talk to them."

Wes closes the door, and we walk toward the motel office. I hesitate for a moment before I open the heavy glass door. A bell rings overhead, and a petite older woman walks out of the backroom. I look into her eyes and see the same greedy look the madam once wore, but this woman's features are different. She's wearing a blazer and large, flashy jewelry which looks out of place in this room.

"How can I help you folks?" She looks at me without recognition, though her gaze is fierce and intimidating.

"Can you tell me about Room 128?"

She takes a breath. "Why?"

"The room is different from the others, and I wondered if there may be a reason why. Just curious, is all."

"Late August 1885, an old bordello called the Bawdy Way burned down in a fire. The building was destroyed, except for that room. My family built around it and repurposed this place into a motel. You can feel the life and energy within that room, so no one could bring themselves to rip it down. Are you interested in staying there?" She reaches behind her for a key.

Wes nudges me with his leg. It's almost as if he fears the door will open on its own and draw him back into his time.

"Yes, actually," I say before I take a quick breath.

Wes glares at me with eyes so fierce, they rival even the madam's. I pay for the room, and the woman drops the key into my hands. I look down and touch the aged metal. A gold tag labeled with the room number hangs from its head.

As we walk toward the room, Wes doesn't look at or speak to me. The muscles of his cheeks pulse from the force of his clenching jaw, and his lips are pressed tight.

I stand in front of room 128, put the key into the lock, and twist it slowly until the lock releases. I ease the door open, and sunlight fills the room. Beyond the threshold waits the familiar old décor and hand-crafted wooden furniture.

Wes looks into the room with a fixed gaze. He's pulled toward the door against his will, as if an invisible rope has wound around his waist. His boot heels grate against the floor as he fights to stay upright. His hands grip both sides of the doorway, his knuckles turning a sickly shade of white. He looks back at me as he grabs the knob and slams the door shut behind him, falling against the wood with a heavy breath. "No, Hannah!"

"Wes, now is your chance to go back!"

"I don't *want* to go back. I thought we already discussed this." He speaks with fire on his tongue, the stern side of

Wes that I've only seen once before. His hands tremble as he gains the strength to stand on his own without bracing against the door. He reaches over and grabs me by my shoulders. "I want to be where *you* are. Whether it's here, there, or somewhere else! I want to stay because I'm happy here. I can sit with you in a cold room when it's a hundred degrees outside. We can get in a car and drive to nowhere and everywhere. There's pizza!" He smiles softly.

"What about what you've lost by coming here?"

"What I've lost? How about what I've gained? I love you, Hannah. I know you're upset about the jewelry, but if you can find it in your heart to forgive me . . . if you can find it in your heart to love me . . . I don't care how hard life is for me here. Can you, Hannah? Can you love me?"

I draw a shaking breath and stare into his eyes. His words are sincere, and they speak to my heart. He's willing to remain in my time to be with me. "That's just it. That isn't even my real name. My name is Mariah. Hannah is a character I play, but I'm sick of acting. I love you, Wes." I drop my shoulders into him and melt into his chest.

"I don't care what your name is, as long as I can call you mine." He pulls me into him and kisses me.

We turn to walk toward the car and nearly crash into the maintenance man as we turn the corner at the west side of the building. His head is down, but he lifts it as we narrowly avoid knocking into him. Red hair sticks out from under his baseball cap, and he looks at me with eerily familiar green eyes. Wes takes several steps back and squares up his stance as the man turns toward us.

"Do I know you?" the man asks, looking at Wes.

"No, definitely not. He's not from around here," I interject.

"Me neither," he says with a solemn voice. He grips the

brim of his hat between his finger and his thumb and tips it toward us as he walks away.

"Wes?" I look at him with a slack-jawed expression.

"I know." Wes watches him until he's out of sight.

"He didn't recognize you, though, so it can't be him," I tell him with a wave of my hand.

Wes cocks his head. "If it ain't him, that was definitely kin of his."

A rumbling sound comes from over our heads, and we look up. An airplane cruises across the sky above us—a bird made of metal and gasoline.

"Is that a plane, Hannah?"

"Yes. Yes, it is."

He stares at it, wraps his arm around my waist, and squeezes me reassuringly, even though I should be the one reassuring him. He's the one giving up his entire life and everything he knows for me.

We reach the car, and Wes opens the passenger door, hesitating for a moment before he sits down. He stares back at the motel room, with its closed and locked door.

I need to accept that Wes is choosing to be here of his own volition. I have to stop pushing him toward that doorway. We can create a life here, even if it's not the one either of us expected. The former whore in me gets excited about the prospect of money and not having to sleep with anyone beside Wes again. Money still drives me, but I suddenly realize that love does as well.

I turn the key in the ignition, and the car roars to life. Wes puts his hand over mine, and we leave the parking lot, hoping we never see the Bawdy Way—in any of its forms —again.

EPILOGUE
WES

I rub my hand along the drywall of the house. It's not my farm, exactly, but it's the bones of it. The haunted moans of my past still call from inside these walls. This house may not be my old farm, but it's a home because of her. Our home.

Air conditioning became a requirement, as did pizza. I whole-heartedly approve of the toilets. Electricity is a wonderful thing, though it doesn't blow my mind as much as it used to.

I worked my way up to ranch manager. Hannah—well, Mariah—finally became the teacher she wanted to be.

I head out into the stifling heat toward the backyard. Wooden fencing snakes along until it almost reaches the cornfield at the end of the property.

I make a kissing sound as I walk. Pounding hoofbeats draw closer as that eerily familiar charcoal mare runs along the fence and meets me by the gate. She nuzzles into me, knocking my hat off my head. I reach down to pick it up and am startled by arms embracing me from behind.

I turn to face Mariah, tipping my hat toward her and pulling her into me. She never holds back when she hugs me, even knowing she'll pull away with dirt and mud on her. She dresses so modern. Her neutral-toned dresses are in stark contrast to my dirty jeans and flannel.

I kiss her left hand, rubbing my finger along the jewel of her ring—a red beryl gemstone. In unsurprising fashion, she didn't want diamonds. She wanted a piece of my past with her at all times.

I have my wife, my horse, and the old farm.

I've had to learn the laws and the customs. The first time Mariah brought home a cat, I damn near clobbered the thing with a broom, thinking it was a varmint. But when it comes down to it, I'd be happy anywhere I ended up, as long as I'm with her. I may not be the man I was, but I'm still the one who will do anything to protect me and mine.

And this is all mine.

Acknowledgments

I am so thankful for my incredibly patient husband who continues to support me on this journey.

A big thank you to my family for accepting me and my stories.

An extra shout out to my uncle, another spectacular writer.

Check out author R.N. Gosser for a fantastic dark fantasy novel debuting in January. She is the best critique partner I could ever ask for!

Lastly, an extra super big acknowledgment to my editor and friend, Brooke, who continues to foster my ideas and help me turn them into masterpieces.

ABOUT THE AUTHOR

Lauren Biel is an author with several titles in the works. When she's not working, she's writing. When she's not writing, she's spending time with her husband, her friends, or her pets. You might also find her on a horseback trail ride or sitting beside a waterfall in Upstate New York. When reading her work, expect the unexpected.

To be the first to know about her upcoming titles, please visit www.LaurenBiel.com.

Never Let Go
Coming Soon

The enemy you lie with isn't always your enemy...

Take another ride on the darker side of things with Lauren Biel's third novel, *Never Let Go*. Enjoy this special preview—an excerpt taken from the first chapter of this upcoming title.

MACKENZIE

A drop of rain splattered on the ground in front of me. I looked up to the sky, hoping the clouds would hold their contents until I could get where I was going. *That's all I need.* Fat drops of rain landed on my shoulders and dripped down my arms. They picked up speed, falling in a curtain illuminated by oncoming headlights. Wind pushed against the growing puddles in the street and guided miniature waves across the asphalt. Mother Nature's response to my silent wish. I shivered as my saturated ponytail directed rivulets down the front of my shirt, sending goosebumps racing along my exposed skin.

The houses blurred together. No matter which way I looked, they all had the same features: big windows and long driveways. Mailboxes lined the road, their numbers nailed to the posts. I picked up the pace to get to the next one. "Shit," I mumbled. The numbers were descending when I needed them to be ascending. The address I was looking for was also odd, not even. Double wrong.

Headlights blinded me as they turned the corner. I started to jog across the street, wanting to walk along the other side. The right side. The speeding car came to a screeching halt, filling the air with the scent of scorched rubber. I apologized with a wave of my hand, and the car sped off as my foot touched down on the opposite sidewalk.

Leaves crackled and swayed overhead. The trees creaked as their trunks moved with the wind. I clutched my purse to my side. *Enough of this.* I dialed my friend's number and put the phone up to my ear. Voicemail.

"Allie! It's Mackenzie. I used the rideshare app and got dropped off down the road. I'm in front of house number... 1936, and it's really dark here. I'm going to head toward the 1990s. If you get this soon, please come get me!"

Fuck. Maybe I should call for another ride. My laziness urged me to do just that—and it *was* tempting—but I kept walking. The streetlights were far apart on this street, and as the darkness built between them, so did the knot in my stomach. My mind played tricks on me in these shadowy places. Footsteps thudded behind me, but every time I swiveled my body, there was only dark concrete and empty space. I shivered.

The bright lights of an oncoming car blinded me, and my eyes clenched shut. It followed beside me at a crawl. I kept my eyes forward, hoping if I didn't acknowledge the driver, they would move along and leave me to find my destination in peace. No such luck. The window lowered with a mechanical whir and revealed the shadow of a woman behind the wheel.

"Do you need a ride?"

ALSO BY LAUREN BIEL

Shoot Down the Stars

"I never knew I was capable of love, hate, distress, and gut wrenching sadness at the same time until I read this book. Proceed with caution."—Beth H.

"I literally loved and hated every character at some point in the book. The emotional impact is just amazing."—Author R.N. Gosser